THE GOOD KNIGHT KISS

D.K. O'Doherty

authorHOUSE®

AuthorHouse™
1663 Liberty Drive
Bloomington, IN 47403
www.authorhouse.com
Phone: 1 (800) 839-8640

Published by AuthorHouse 12/06/2017

ISBN: 978-1-5462-1916-3 (sc)
ISBN: 978-1-5462-1915-6 (e)

Print information available on the last page.

This book is printed on acid-free paper.

Scriptures are taken from the King James Version
of The Bible - Public Domain.

CHAPTER 1

he forest animals heard the din of the hoofbeats bearing down on them. Daniel pressed Macha. The huge Frisian warhorse had extraordinary speed and endurance, even for a Frisian, which were bred to carry the German knights during the most recent Crusades. Daniel's mastiff, Balor, matched the speed and endurance of the black horse. The three had often traveled from encampment to battlefield over the years, but the horse and dog sensed that Daniel's anxiety had to do with something other than an impending battle.

It began to rain, and the gentle breeze felt like a gale as the pace of horse and rider quickened. The raindrops pelted Daniel's face. Gusts of wind pushed tree branches into the path of the three companions. Numerous cuts riddled Daniel's face and exposed skin. Daniel felt Macha's heart thump against his legs. The thunder of hooves against the well-traveled road drowned out all the forest sounds and gave fair warning to any animals in the path to flee. Several forest smells entered Daniel's nostrils. If not for the urgency of the situation, he would have slowed Macha to enjoy each scent. The rain tasted sweet.

The trees became a blur as the companions raced faster. The forest consisted of a magnificent blend of tall, thick pine, oak, birch, and aspen. This forest was just as extensive as other forests throughout Ireland. Each season revealed the unique beauty of the Irish forests, but the loudest forest sounds occurred in summer. Birds, animals, and travelers all contributed. In autumn, the leaves and needles of the trees floated gently to the forest floor, providing a carpet to muffle the sounds of hoofbeats and carriage wheels. Winter caused many of the deciduous trees to slumber. Some animals joined the trees in hibernation, while most birds traveled south to warmer climates until spring called them home. That spring arrived typically late. March could never decide when to let go of winter's embrace.

The early rain passed, and the fog lingered on the village of Lough Inch. So the emergence of Daniel and his two companions out of the forest through the cold, gray mist caused quite a disturbance. The villagers who faced the forest edge believed they witnessed the return of one of the ancient giants. Daniel stood over six feet tall and weighed over 230 pounds. His braided brown hair and beard complemented his piercing green eyes. They showed a man of high intelligence who had witnessed the many wonders and the many horrors this world offered. He wore the standard armor of knights of the fourteenth century. Daniel carried a broadsword across his back, two daggers on his belt, a short sword sheathed on the left side of the saddle, and a mace on the right; a round shield rested comfortably on his left arm. Around his neck, an opal dangled from a leather thong.

The Opal Knight atop the Frisian warhorse put his helm at over nine and a half feet from the ground. The sight of the knight and horse at full gallop, with the mastiff alongside, caused many villagers to stop their tasks and stare in awe, but their awe gave way to fear as they observed the three covering the distance from forest edge to village in a short time. They entered the village at full gallop.

Lough Inch was a small village on the verge of becoming a decent-size town. It sat on the banks of a lake, on which the village relied heavily for survival. The entire culture of the village revolved around the lake. Many thatched cottages dotted Lough Inch. Except for a select few, all the cottages looked identical, and only the inhabitants knew the social status of the populace. The typical cottage consisted of a thatched roof, single door, two windows—one always faced east—and a small yard or garden. Not many other features distinguished one from another. The village also contained the usual structures that gave a village its charm.

The village blacksmith owned the stable. The blacksmith did well for himself. Aside from shoeing horses, he made and repaired various weapons and armor for the local garrison. Daniel often sought the blacksmith's expertise to repair a damaged sword or dented armor. The local garrison consisted of thirty to forty men, depending on the season. During the planting and harvest seasons, the garrison dropped to the minimum. A sergeant of the guard and captain rounded it out.

The marketplace stood centrally located within the village. Soon after its establishment, the tavern developed into the centerpiece of local gossip and goings-on throughout the country. Many travelers sought the tavern for a meal and a drink and often remained overnight in one of the rooms in the back. If one wanted to find out what had happened recently or was about to happen, he visited the tavern for a few pints. A brothel, once popular, had been connected to the tavern but no longer existed in this town. The tavern owner now rented the rooms for overnights to travelers.

A small church occupied a small parcel of land on the edge of the village opposite the lake. Although small in stature, the church wielded an incredible amount of influence throughout the country, and Lough Inch was no exception.

Daniel and his companions entered the town in a rush of hooves and paws. His destination was a thin plume of black smoke, swirling up at the opposite end of the village from where he entered. They hastened at a pace too fast for the townspeople. Daniel weaved Macha through the throng in the marketplace. He even failed to pause after Macha and Balor knocked over several carts and tables. Many of the villagers turned to yell at the lunatic, but on recognizing the Opal Knight, they hesitated. The villagers all knew the reason for the recklessness. Balor always took the lead in tight places such as the village. His deep, guttural barking caused people to move before the great horse barreled them over, generally causing few injuries. Occasionally, Balor nipped at the calves of those who failed to heed his barking.

As Daniel neared the source of the smoke, the odor became stronger. He smelled the burned thatch and wood. And as the wind shifted, he recognized the smell of something unpleasant—an odor that had become all too familiar during the many sieges he had participated in, both as attacker and defender. With the recognition of the odor, those long-buried memories rushed to the surface. His mind became cluttered with the recollections of the burned flesh of those brave soldiers who had attempted to crash through the drawbridge of a castle as the fiery pitch poured down from castle ramparts. The pitch clung to their clothing and bare skin, eventually searing through to the bone.

The screams grew louder as he neared the devastation, except they did not come from his memories. They came from Daniel. He screamed in fear. Daniel screamed, feeling helpless. Macha felt the panic in her rider. She pulled to a stop without a command from Daniel. The Opal Knight bolted out of the saddle and charged into the smoldering remains of the cottage.

"You killed her! You killed her!"

Balor barked with fury and anger. Anger at whom? Himself for allowing his master to risk his life? Or at his master for not having any sense?

Macha pawed the ground with her great hooves, throwing up huge clods of earth.

Daniel's eyes watered from the heat and ash. His nostrils flared from the smell of burned flesh, and his hands burned and blistered as he dug through the searing rubble, looking for her in desperation. The smoldering embers sizzled as they sought more fuel. Daniel felt something behind him, but he dismissed it. He had to find her.

Several hands grabbed the huge knight and tried to pull him to safety. Daniel shrugged off the pulling hands and continued his desperate search. More hands grabbed the Opal Knight. It took four villagers pulling his arms and torso and two pushing from the front to subdue him. The villagers pushed him against the huge oak tree across the road from where her cottage once stood. He slumped to the ground, his back supported by the trunk of the oak. Only two days earlier, he had emerged from the same forest but not headed into Lough Inch.

Two days prior, the Opal Knight had appeared out of the forest atop Macha and headed into Galway. Macha, not the typical warhorse deployed in Ireland, stood at least one and a half times as tall as and outweighed every standard warhorse used throughout the land by three hundred pounds. Balor, his other companion, trotted ahead, sniffing out potential danger.

Macha belonged to the breed Frisian. The beautiful, black Frisians were renowned for their reputation for carrying the Frisian and German knights great distances during the Crusades. Macha represented her Frisian breed well. An immense and powerful horse even for her breed, Macha stood sixteen hands at the withers and weighed over seventeen hundred pounds. Her long, thick, black mane and tail were braided in much the same fashion as her rider's braided beard and hair.

Balor, the huge brown mastiff, stood thirty-two inches at the shoulder and weighed as much as his master. The ideal guard and protector, Balor took his role seriously. If he even minutely sensed that someone or something intended to harm his master, it never ended well for that particular threat.

Many townspeople stared in awe at the splendor and magnificence of the Opal Knight riding the Frisian and the mastiff, trotting alongside effortlessly. The three could quickly cover long distances in a short period of time. Although the edge of the forest was at least a half mile away from the port city of Galway, within a few minutes, the three companions had arrived at the edge of the town.

A bustling merchant town, Galway rested on the western coast of Ireland, between Donegal to the north and Kerry to the south. If one rode due east for approximately 110 miles, Dublin would be reached in about five days. With easy access to the Atlantic, the sea became a primary source of food for much of the town.

As the knight and his companions entered the town, it became all too evident that Galway was a fishing port. Balor sneezed uncontrollably from the stench of rotting fish. In one corner of the market square, discarded parts of numerous species of fish piled high. Two townsfolk routinely shoveled the pile into a cart. They then pulled it down to the bay, tipped it up, and dumped the cart contents off the dock into the ocean, where other fish would then gobble up the chunks.

The townspeople doddered about their daily lives, eking out a means to survive. Some worked the docks, while others sold fish, meat, vegetables, or anything else someone might buy in the market. Local constables maintained the peace. The monks from the abbey made themselves available to give the faithful their daily lesson of guilt for being alive. Over all of them ruled the local king. The king maintained order and called up citizens in times of trouble. Some kings also had at their disposal mercenaries and knights to help defend their land from the threat of invasion from Vikings and attacks from the English or even from neighboring kings.

As a Knight of the Realm, it was Daniel's sworn duty to defend his king's land when summoned. Two days earlier, the church elders of Lough Inch had read aloud a decree from the king summoning the services of all men of fighting age to defend the main port of Galway from a Viking invasion. Sworn to hasten immediately to his king's aid, Daniel readied immediately; however, upon saying farewell to the love of his life, he hesitated. Something deep down bothered him. She knew it too. She felt Daniel's hesitance, but she also knew he was a knight, the Opal Knight. She held his hand with her left and placed her right hand gently against his left cheek. A warm tear rolled down his cheek onto her fingers. He did not want to go again. He did not want to leave her again. Cassandra looked up into those eyes she loved so much, the green eyes of the gentle giant she had grown to love. She had fallen in love with him over and over again, and those eyes always revealed to her the true Danny. Cassandra's Danny was kind and gentle, yet powerful and strong. Danny was her protector, but she also knew that if the Vikings attacked again, they would not leave right away. The Viking presence would devastate this land, its people, the animals, and the magic. Yes, she must let Danny go. Galway did not stand a chance without him; with Danny, Galway stood an even chance of survival.

The memory faded as Daniel gazed confused out beyond the bay. The sea remained calm and empty. Not one Viking raider appeared on the horizon. The townspeople mulled about as if it were a typical day, not as if they expected a raid soon. Where were the call-ups? Where were the other knights? Assuredly, he was not the first to arrive in response to his king's summons. It had taken him three days to travel from his village. Certainly other knights lived closer and should have arrived sooner than he. The townspeople gave way as he entered the square, wary of Balor as he bared his teeth. This was the only warning necessary to any who might wish his master harm.

"Excuse me, friend," Daniel said, interrupting one of the citizens shoveling fish remnants into his cart. He could have asked any of the locals, but experience had taught him to always seek out the one everyone ignores, the one who performs the most lowly, disgusting task but without whom life for everyone else would be difficult to endure. This person usually had some of the most vital pieces of information.

"Yes, sir, knight."

"What is the latest report on the Viking raiders?"

"Viking raiders? There is no report. There has not been a Viking raid in Ireland in over 150 years."

"Yeah, but the village elders had valuable information from reliable sources that the Vikings had gained strength and power again. They were traveling their old invasion routes looking to begin pillaging and plundering all over again."

"Sir, I am sorry you have been misinformed. There has never been a Viking raid on Galway. Look out there. Do you see any raiders?"

"I can see!" Daniel's anger surfaced, but he had it under great control. *Why would the church elders lie to me?* he thought. *Why would they want me away from the village for so long? What could they possibly gain from my absence? It doesn't make any sense. I am the Opal Knight. I am the village protector. I have saved countless lives since arriving there and settling down with my true ...* The knight continued in his thoughts, *No! It cannot be. But yes, that is the only explanation.*

Daniel turned Macha around and bolted through the market toward the forest where he had appeared just an hour earlier. Balor ran alongside. Daniel's stress caused internal anguish. When he felt anguish this strong, his mind pushed forward the memories of how he had met the three most important souls in his life. Both of his companions had been with Daniel for a long time, and the circumstances surrounding their meetings were quite unique.

Macha was born very small for her breed. She did not even have a name for the first two years of her life. Her mother took care of her the best she could, but eventually there came a time for Macha to be sold. Unfortunately, Macha was first sold to a farmer. That did not work well for either. Macha became bored and refused to pull the plow. The irritated farmer beat Macha until, tired of the whip, she would begin her boring task again of pulling the rusted plow through the clods of mud and dirt in the heat of the sun. Eventually, the farmer became weary of the constant struggle with his horse. Times were bad enough without having to deal with a stubborn horse that refused to work. So, after one season, the farmer sold the Frisian to a traveling merchant pulling a huge cart of his wares. The merchant had all sorts of items and trinkets. It seemed there was something for everyone, except weapons and armor. These items remained under the control of each village garrison. One could hear the cart long before it arrived. The clanging of the metal objects and squeaking of the wheels gave away its approach long before one saw it.

Macha had no idea that the merchant had bought her. Whether hitched to the plow or cart, the boredom never ceased. The steady sting of the reins on her back or the occasional whip against her rump became part of the routine. The merchant gave her a name—actually, three names to choose from: Beast, Horse, or Stupid. It wasn't until the spring when Macha finally found her calling. The merchant drove her into another town and set up his cart in the marketplace. She remained, as always, hitched to the cart while the merchant bartered. This particular morning a rather tall man approached her. He was dressed in strange clothing that had a familiar smell to it. His clothes smelled wonderful. She did not recognize all the scents, but they were wonderful and triggered something deep inside her, something she had not felt since she was a young foal. She wanted freedom. She wanted to run. He smiled at her, and her ears and head perked up. His hand touched the side of her face. At the movement of the stranger's hand, Macha jerked away in expectation of another beating, but something about this man set him apart from the others she had served. He made Macha feel calm and at peace as his right hand gently stroked the left side of her face. His words soothed her also.

"You are a beautiful animal. You look so strong and full of life. Why are you being tormented working as a puller of trinkets?"

The man walked toward the merchant, tapped him on the shoulder, and asked, "Excuse me, how much for that fine animal?"

The merchant was attempting to sell something of no value for much more than what it was worth to an unwary patron. "What? I'm busy. Come back later."

"I asked how much for your horse," the man repeated.

"And I said I was busy. Now get away from me or I will be forced to …" The merchant stopped talking as he turned and came face to chest with the huge knight.

"Forced to what?" the knight asked in a much different tone than before.

"Um, err …"

"That's what I thought. Now, you can adopt a more civil tone of voice with me, or we can proceed down a path I'm sure you will not enjoy. It's your choice."

Distracted by the huge knight, the merchant failed to

observe his patron seize the opportunity to snatch one of the silver spoons off the table and walk away.

The merchant heeded the knight's advice and changed his tone. "I'm sorry, sir. I must have mistaken you for some wretch off the street, but obviously I was mistaken."

"Indeed. How much for your horse?"

"Why do you want it?"

"It does not matter why. All that matters is that you ask a fair price or I may come to the conclusion that you are a cheater and swindler. As a duly appointed knight, it would certainly be my duty to inform the baron of this town of that fact. We all know what happens to such criminals in this country."

The merchant mulled this over for a few moments and came to the conclusion that this horse was stupid and stubborn anyway. Ever seeking a profit, the merchant tried his luck. "This is a fine animal, a strong beast. I will be hard pressed to find another like him."

"Her. This fine animal is a female."

The merchant shook his head in agreement. "Of course—her, sir. Even better, she will produce splendid offspring. Not only that, but I will now either have to find another beast or pull the cart myself. I'm afraid the price … the compensation for such a great loss may be too high even for you."

"How much?"

"One hundred fifty gold pieces!"

"Fifteen."

"Ninety, and I cannot go any lower."

"Twenty-five."

"Impossible."

"This horse has been abused and treated unfairly for so long. I am offering a fair deal."

"That's the way I got it."

"Her. Not it."

"Whatever. Either way, ninety gold pieces is my final offer."

"I see. I thought you might be difficult," Daniel said, moving toward the merchant.

"Wait. Wait. Forty?" the merchant offered, waving his hands.

"Twenty-five." Daniel moved a step closer.

"Sold! You drive a hard bargain, knight."

The merchant received the twenty-five gold pieces in his left hand and put out his right as a gesture of good will. Daniel looked at him with disgust. The merchant felt it best to back away before he pushed his luck one too many times.

Since she was trussed to the cart of merchant wares, Macha only heard an exchange of words behind her. She smelled the big man nearing her and felt his large, gentle hand rubbing her side. She also felt the chains and harness removed. Macha felt relieved. It seemed as though they never were off. Her skin and coat were worn down by the constant rubbing of the rough leather. The sores burned, but it was a small price to pay to feel the relief of the old leather. She observed the face of the large man through her big, brown, almond-shaped eyes and noticed drops of water running from his eyes and down his cheeks as he removed the bit from her mouth.

"Don't worry. Daniel is here now," he said. "You will be strong and healthy again."

The three companions crashed into the forest and found the trail that led back home to Lough Inch. The tall and thick trees of the forest were a magnificent blend of pine, oak, birch, and aspen. The extensive forest protected many species of animals, as well as the occasional band of highwaymen. This forest was similar to many of the forests throughout Ireland. They looked beautiful in all seasons, each of which had its unique qualities. The forest was filled with the loudest sounds during summer. Many people traveled the forest to get from one village to the other when the roads allowed for ease of footing. Disorganized highwaymen roved the forests and used them for protection. They posed no real threat to any other than the lone traveler. In autumn, the trees released their leaves and needles, which floated gently to the ground and trails below. The covering muffled the sounds of the hoofbeats of horses and the wheels of carriages. The winter, of course, caused many of the deciduous trees to sleep. Some animals joined the trees in hibernation waiting for the call of spring. As a youth, Daniel had traveled all the forests of Ireland while under the tutelage of nontraditional experts.

Daniel pushed Macha, knowing her endurance would not falter for a while. Balor could keep pace just as long. Macha and Balor both felt the tension from their master and pushed themselves even harder. The sun quickly descended below the horizon. Soon the night would reign upon the entire land. Both horse and dog could easily traverse the terrain of the dark forest with their keen eyesight to guide them. Macha certainly would not allow her rider to fall, but something about the night always bothered Daniel. Before darkness enveloped them, Daniel paused on the edge of a clearing in the middle of the forest and hastily built a fire. The fire appeared disproportionate to the area and size of the party. He had intentionally built the fire so. He required light all around him.

Macha and Balor did not comprehend why complete darkness terrified Daniel, but it did not matter to them. Macha just wanted to stay close to her master and protect him in the only way she knew how. Balor owed Daniel the same level of respect and loyalty, especially considering the peculiar circumstance in which they had met.

As one of six pups in a litter born to a stray, there was not much use for him or his litter mates in the small Alsatian town bordering Germany and France. The townspeople tried to rid the area of all stray animals, which they believed became harbingers of evil and the spies of witches. Other than just being slain by the local guards' swords, the strays faced a threat from the Burgermeister, who considered it a more profitable venture to sell the strays to the local arena for entertainment. Unfortunately for the strays, the amusement consisted of anything from being sparring partners for juveniles learning the basics of the arena to serving as prey for any number of exotic animals brought home as trophies of conquest.

Balor and his litter mates sat cramped in a cage just outside the arena. Wrought with hunger, they received just enough rations to keep them alive. The pups whined from hunger, thirst, or lying and sitting in their own filth.

On foot, Daniel led Macha through the crowd toward the arena. He had heard rumors of this arena and had to see for himself if they held any truth. It never ceased to disgust Daniel the inhumanity that humans inflicted on the creatures of this world. Now, as he approached the arena, it became all too clear that the rumors were true. Cages contained various exotic and local animals destined as entertainment for the masses. Daniel's temper grew, and Macha felt his anger. She pressed her face closer so that he could feel her; he lifted his hand to her face and patted her cheek.

"Don't worry, Macha. I'm not going to do anything rash, but don't you think that these beasts are being treated harshly? They certainly deserve to have a fighting chance." With that last statement, a sly grin appeared on Daniel's face.

Daniel released Macha's reins so he could work quicker and more efficiently, but Macha remained close to her master. Daniel walked up and down the menagerie of exotic and local animals and unlocked their cages. First one and then another beast pushed open their cage doors. As the creatures realized that the unlocked doors of their enclosures led to freedom, they exited. Soon, the holding area filled with lions, tigers, wolves, boars, dogs, bears, and strange birds—all hungry and angry. Daniel may not have saved all of those beautiful animals, and many even died that day, but they died free and fighting. Daniel nodded with approval as the large predators sought vengeance on their tormentors. The throng of onlookers panicked, and Daniel left the mayhem.

On the edge of the town, as Daniel proceeded to mount Macha, he heard tiny footsteps from behind. He turned and expected to confront a town official or, worse, an arena guard, but there was no one. He looked down, and sitting at his feet was one of the mastiff puppies he had set free. A smile appeared on Daniel's face, and he knew the pup had just selected him. He reached down, picked up the pup, and placed him on the saddle.

Balor sat close to Daniel and felt the warmth of the fire. The smell of the hardtack Daniel carried with him caused the mastiff to drool, and Daniel broke off a piece to share with his friend. Macha busied herself grazing on the perimeter of the meadow. She still kept a wary eye and ear for any danger. Daniel's two companions worked favorably together to protect their master. Macha always assumed the responsibility of the outer defense and early warning, while Balor protected the inner circle and remained close to Daniel while he slept. Soon after Daniel and Balor devoured their meals, both settled down for what would be a restless night filled with tossing, turning, and nightmares of what had happened to Cassandra. Balor whimpered every time Daniel called out, empathizing with his restlessness. Macha would wake from her light sleep to quickly determine whether there was an immediate threat. With none detected, she would let out a *harrumph* and go back to sleep. Throughout the night, Daniel continued to toss and turn, and Macha and Balor remained ever vigilant. Although both companions appeared to sleep soundly, upon closer examination both remained alert. Their ears were in constant motion, picking up every sound the forest made available to them.

Daniel woke early, before sunrise. He took account of all of his equipment and looked for her. There she was, as always, finishing her nightly trek across sky. The full moon always comforted Daniel, and he did not truly understand or appreciate the power she had over every living thing on earth until Cassandra had showed him years earlier. He had to get to her before any of his nightmares came true. Balor stepped from the forest edge and made his way to Daniel. Daniel petted his friend and gave a low whistle for Macha to join them. As she arrived, Daniel stepped close to say good morning. He then broke off another piece of hardtack for Balor. Daniel smothered the fire with dirt and saddled Macha for the ride ahead.

The sun continued to rise, and the higher it rose, the more light appeared, helping Daniel feel comfortable away from the fire. He pressed Macha. The huge warhorse had extraordinary speed and endurance, which could be matched by Balor. The three had often traveled in this manner from encampment to battlefield over the years, but the horse and dog felt that Daniel's anxiety this time was due to something other than the excitement of battle.

The grief Daniel suffered prevented him from recognizing the pain from his blistered hands.

CHAPTER 2

efeated, Daniel sat on the ground with his back against the magnificent oak, his legs bent and forearms resting on his knees. His head was bent toward his chest, his shoulders shook uncontrollably, and he muttered, "She's dead. She's dead. You killed her. You killed her. *I killed her!*"

Both horse and dog loved their knight and tried their best to comfort him. Macha nuzzled her master, and Balor ran up and licked the tears from Daniel's face. A raven circled overhead and perched on a branch about twenty feet above the ground. With great interest, the raven observed the goings-on.

As the crowd of onlookers grew, the men who had pulled the knight from the destroyed cottage melted into the throng. A few women stepped forward to assist and comfort Daniel, but Macha and Balor moved in to intercept them. Daniel did not receive any assistance from the villagers that day. An unshod little girl stepped through the crowd unnoticed. Macha and Balor parted and let her pass between them toward their master. She wore a frayed, green dress with a ringlet of flowers around her head. A single ornament dangled from a necklace about her neck as she bent and tended to Daniel's hands. She applied a salve and dressed his wounds. As she finished the last wrap, the little girl whispered unintelligible words to Daniel. She placed her hand on the knight's shoulder and comforted him. Daniel's physical pain subsided, but his mental anguish lingered.

As Daniel lifted his head, he spoke, "The love of my life is gone. She is dead. I should have stayed. I could have protected her. She was so beautiful and innocent. She never hurt anyone or anything. She was perfect—a saint."

The villagers murmured derogatory comments, and a self-appointed spokesman stepped forward, interrupting the Opal Knight's remorse. "How dare you speak of that witch as if she were a princess! She was not a *saint*! She was *not innocent! She was evil!*"

Daniel simmered and stood to his full height and towered over the villagers around him. The little girl rose and stepped back, thus clearing a straight path from the knight to the mob. He was a full head taller than the stoutest man in the crowd. Several paces behind Daniel, the huge warhorse and battle dog moved toward the village mob in seismic rhythm with the knight's steps. The mob knew the capabilities of the knight when he was in a good mood as well as when enraged. The Opal Knight appeared as a giant from ancient times compared to the spokesman. As the knight approached, everyone nearby heard his knuckles crack as he clenched his fists tighter and tighter. The mob realized its mistake and backed away. Injured and unarmed, Daniel easily outmatched any of the villagers. Considering his warhorse and battle dog, those in the mob convinced themselves that their wives or children were calling them home. They left the self-appointed spokesman to face his fate alone.

Daniel stopped inches from the spokesman and bent over so that he was eye to eye with him. "There are several options I have at my disposal. I could strangle you. I could pummel your body with my fists until you forget your name. I could let my friends here loose on you. But you are not worth my time or my energy, you piece of dung."

The spokesman shook uncontrollably, realizing how close he had come to being ripped apart and fed to the knight's dog. He felt something warm on his legs, looked down, and discovered that he had involuntarily relieved himself. He then watched in fear as the massive dog stepped inches from his chest, snarled, bared his teeth, lifted his right rear leg, and relieved himself on the spokesman as well.

The knight turned and headed out of town toward the ancient ruins on the hill on the outskirts of the village. Macha and Balor followed and kept vigilant watch over their master. The raven flew ahead as if it understood the Opal Knight's destination.

For centuries, the locals had referred to the ancient circle on the outskirts of the village as the Mound, and Daniel headed toward it. He walked with a purpose driven by anger. However, the wind shifted, and the aroma of the burning embers fueled by the remains of the cottage filled his nostrils. His pace slowed. His shoulders slumped, and he collapsed in defeat. Daniel pounded the ground and cried in despair. He slouched over and dragged himself through the muddy road. Neither of his companions had ever seen their master in such a state. Confused and concerned, Macha paced in a circle, while Balor crawled next to the knight. Daniel soon stopped dragging himself and laid face down in the brown, soupy mud. Balor rested his chin on Daniel's back. The sky darkened, and the clouds swirled. Shortly, rain came down in heavy drops, pounding the three friends. Macha and Balor endured the rain. They would not leave Daniel. He continued to cry even as puddles formed around and under him.

Daniel's sobbing ebbed, but he still lay there in the muddy puddle of water mixed with his sweat and tears.

He felt a slight tug at his arm. At first, he thought Balor or Macha was pulling at him, but he felt the grip of small fingers, not teeth. The grip seemed to be that of a small person—a woman or child—and it felt strong yet gentle. The small hand pulled Daniel until he was on all fours. As he rose, the fire opal attached to the leather strap placed around his neck so many years ago dangled outside of his shirt. Daniel grasped the opal and felt the energy, emotions, and memories connected with it. He heard a slight whisper that demanded, "Get up, knight! Your armor is dented, *not* broken."

Although his crying had subsided, irregular bouts of remorseful weeping crept to the surface, and the sobbing would start over. With the aid of the small hand, Daniel lifted himself to his knees and surveyed his surroundings. Balor sat nearby, and Macha circled the three. Because of the extreme sorrow of losing his love and the somber thoughts brought on from the crying, Daniel did not consider asking the boy's name, where he came from, or how the boy had approached him without warning from Balor and Macha. Balor never took to strangers right away, especially those who approached his master without being introduced; however, the presence of the boy calmed even the suspicious mastiff.

The child walked around and faced Daniel. Since Daniel knelt, the boy faced Daniel eye to eye. Daniel peered deeply into the child's eyes. The eyes told one everything he or she needed to know; they expressed happiness, sadness, anger, deceit, truth—the entire gambit of emotions and thoughts. One had to have received training to delve deep into the mind and soul behind the glimmer of the eyes. Daniel had received this specialized training a few years after meeting her. This particular training had prevented many misunderstandings in the past. Because he was so adept at this art, generals and kings often brought Daniel in to resolve arguments before they escalated into regional conflicts. People often misinterpreted words and deeds, but the eyes never lied. The eyes always told the truth. Daniel continued to look past the boy's gray eyes, beyond the innocence of youth, but he could not push any deeper than the surface of those eyes. He had the eyes of a boy, but not.

"Daniel?"

No response.

"Sir, knight?"

Dazed look.

"Opal Knight?"

This shook Daniel from his staring. "How do you know that name?"

"It's obvious. When your shoulders hunched over, the opal necklace around your neck appeared from under your shirt."

"Oh. Who are you? Where did you come from? I've never seen you around here before. I know everyone in these parts, including the children."

"Those are irrelevant questions and nonsensical facts. Daniel, you must get up. You cannot quit."

"Quit? *Quit?* I'm a Knight of the Realm. I do not quit. But what's the point of going on?" Daniel asked, looking down. "My love is dead."

"She is gone, but you are still her knight."

Daniel lifted his head, and the boy had vanished. Balor and Macha acted as if the boy had never been there.

Daniel thought, *The boy was right. I am a knight. I am*

the Opal Knight. I am her *knight! She is gone, but I will right this injustice. I will seek out those who have done this and avenge Cassandra's murder!*

Daniel tucked the opal necklace back inside his shirt where it had been since the moment she placed it around his neck. At the age of five, Daniel had first seen Cassandra. Not much older than Daniel, she appeared smaller and thinner than the other children of the village. As a child, Cassandra had short, curly brown hair. She had an unusual olive tone to her skin—not the creamy, white skin tone of the inhabitants native to Ireland. Cassandra always seemed adorably clumsy. She appeared to continually drop some item she carried or stumble for no reason throughout the day. This clumsiness followed her into adulthood. Many of the children throughout the village teased Cassandra about her appearance and clumsiness, but Daniel had never seen any girl or woman more beautiful.

Daniel gazed upon the opal and recalled the first time Cassandra spoke to him. As a boy, he would sneak out of his house to explore the village and surrounding countryside. As the village grew and became organized, more and more cottages and town buildings filled open parcels of land. They formed alleys and shortcuts from one end of town to the other, thus decreasing travel time for anyone attempting to get around unnoticed. The first time Daniel laid his eyes on her, he had just made his way down a dark alley. As he maneuvered his way around the refuse and wooden barrels on the other side of the road, he noticed for the first time the most beautiful home in the village. He had heard of a beautiful cottage somewhere on the other side of the village, but, as much as he had searched for it, he never could find it until that moment; coincidentally, it was also the first time he saw Cassandra. Instantly smitten by her, Daniel made it a point from that moment to visit her every day for several weeks. Because of his unusual shyness around girls, Daniel's visits became more of a furtive reconnaissance mission. An old tree stump became his favorite observation post; he hid behind it at a safe distance, undetected by her.

From the first time Daniel saw his Cassandra, he thought he concealed himself perfectly from her view. Circumstances at home dictated that Daniel become adept at making himself vanish into the shadows, so he was sure Cassandra could not see him. Unbeknownst to him, however, Cassandra had the capability to see him before he saw her.

He approached his usual hiding place. There he crouched down into his concealed position to watch Cassandra read a huge book. Bound in leather and worn by continuous use over many years, it was the same book she read every day. When she sat on the bench outside her front door to read, the book concealed her entire lap. Daniel noticed that Cassandra wore dresses of such bright, vivid colors that they competed with the beauty of the garden. She wore a different colored dress every day and had dresses with each color of the rainbow. Daniel didn't recall her ever wearing white, brown, or black during that time. He discovered the reason later.

Cassandra lived in the same cottage her entire life, the same cottage that now smoldered in ruin. Young saplings surrounded the property, which quickly grew into many of the giant oaks that still stood. Many varieties of flowers, vegetables, and bushes adorned the humble grounds and garden, some of which Daniel knew and had heard of, such as roses, lilacs, potatoes, carrots, onions, mulberry, and gooseberry. Many others he could not pronounce and were not from this land. As he matured, he learned that these strange plants served purposes other than food and beauty.

Thatch-roofed cottages occupied by poor families dotted the village among the intermittent buildings that supported town life. The entire village considered Cassandra's dwelling unique. Thatched like the rest of the village, Cassandra's cottage had two chimneys instead of one. It always seemed to be in perfect condition and never needed repairs. Unlike the drab-looking cottages, Cassandra's picturesque cottage stood out. Dyed with very bright colors, the doors and shutters grabbed the immediate attention of everyone within eyesight. The front door was colored purple, and the back door was a bright orange. The window frames alternated in blue, green, red, and yellow. A knee-high stone wall protected the cottage, and the bright green grass in the back had no comparison in the village. A deadly sin dominated the thoughts of many village women. Jealousy became a fixture among them. Their jealousy of the little girl's cottage grew with good reason. The squalid condition of all the rest of the cottages in the village made it impossible to differentiate between the poorest and wealthiest residents. Their husbands always compared their cottage to Cassandra's, wondering out loud why they could not have a nice cottage also.

Each morning, Cassandra's mum, Iliana, ventured outside the cottage to tend the garden and to walk the perimeter of their parcel of land with her daughter. Sometimes, mother and daughter paused to whisper something together near different sections of the stone wall.

When not tending the garden or whispering, Iliana always yelled at Cassandra to stop daydreaming, tend to her chores, or study. Cassandra's father did not live with them, and, of course, numerous rumors spread quickly as to why.

The day Daniel heard her voice for the first time, he had gone about his usual routine. However, upon settling into his hiding position, he did not see Cassandra.

Where could she be? he thought. *Is something wrong?*

Young Daniel's imagination took control of his senses and emotions. *Is she sick? Was she kidnapped by a roving band of leprechauns? Giants? Perhaps, worst of all, she moved away.*

He panicked. Something terrible had befallen Daniel's secret love. He had to rescue his fair maiden. Daniel leapt up, freed his dagger from its sheath, and prepared for battle. Cassandra's cottage and garden looked as they always did— pristine, clean, and in perfect condition. He expected to see the garden trampled, the walls knocked down, and the front door kicked open with Cassandra's mother crying hysterically, but nothing indicated that any evil doer had attacked the cottage. Everything seemed as it always did, except there was no Cassandra. Daniel tried to climb over the wall but found that he could not. He had proven himself the best climber in the village over and over again, yet he failed to scale the wall. How could he not scale a wall not even as high as his waist?

He walked around the perimeter searching for his maiden. Daniel used his keen eyesight to scan up into the trees and behind the bushes in case Cassandra lay unconscious or incapacitated. He could not locate her anywhere. He considered calling out to her but thought better of it. What if the fiends still lurked about? As he made his way back toward the front of the house, he heard a cute, tiny giggle from where the little girl usually sat. Cassandra sat on the bench by the purple front door as she always had since that first day, and every day since in the weeks that followed. There she sat with the huge tome on her lap as if nothing had happened, giggling.

"You are funny."

Daniel stopped, stunned. He thought he heard her. Did Cassandra just talk to him? He stood there and stared at the prettiest girl he had ever seen up close. Daniel had often imagined how her voice sounded. Each day in his hiding spot, he hoped it didn't sound like all the other girls in the village. They annoyed him with their teasing and loud, high-pitched screeches they called voices. Daniel often referred to the girls as a herd of bleating goats. Cassandra's voice seemed not to have a sound, if possible. Her voice reminded him of the gentle ripples on the surface of a pond as a pebble breaks its surface. It sounded better than he had ever imagined. Her voice floated on the air as a soft feather drifts down to the earth.

Daniel stammered the only thing that came to mind. "H-h-h-hi."

Cassandra giggled louder this time. "You're cute."

He took a step toward the wall and hoped this time he could climb over it. The cottage door swung open, and Cassandra's mother, Iliana, stood in the doorway. She frowned and folded her arms across her chest.

"Cassandra, what have I told you about practicing where they could see you?"

The way Iliana said *they* gave Daniel the feeling that she disliked him. Cassandra started and closed her book. "But, Mom, I like him. He is funny and cute."

"I don't care! Get inside *now*!"

Cassandra stomped off, but as she entered the house, she gave a quick glance over her shoulder, smiled, and winked at Daniel. After Cassandra went inside, Iliana closed the door and approached Daniel. She stopped directly opposite the side of the wall where he stood.

"Do not come around here anymore, little boy. You are a menace and a distraction. My daughter has a lot of studying to do." Iliana turned to go inside.

"Umm, ma'am?"

"What!" Iliana stopped and faced Daniel.

"I noticed that your daughter is a princess. She is a princess without a knight to protect her. Since I am *not* a little boy but a knight in training, I offer my services as your daughter's personal protector." Daniel removed his cap and bowed as he finished providing his offering.

Iliana took a step, hesitated, whispered something, turned, and went into the cottage.

Daniel backed away from the wall, terrified. As the door closed, he heard Cassandra and Iliana scream at each other but did not understand the words. He wanted to rescue his princess from her mother but knew he could not at this time. Instead, he crept back into the shadows of his hiding place. Daniel remained there in hopes he might speak with Cassandra again. He felt a compulsion to leave, but he fought it back into the depths of his mind. Daniel and Cassandra continued to see each other in secret throughout their childhood and into their young adult lives. They learned many things from each other and together.

CHAPTER 3

Balor barked twice, and Daniel broke his gaze upon the opal. He placed it back inside his shirt, touching his chest where his heartbeat kept it warm. Daniel looked up into the sky, took a deep breath, staggered to his feet, and continued his walk up the hill toward the Mound with his companions. HIs thoughts intermittently switched back and forth to happier times with his love and then back to only a few hours earlier, when he dug through the burning remains of the cottage. Daniel had so many questions and no answers to any of them.

Balor scouted ahead for potential danger as Macha stayed close to Daniel. When the small group finally arrived at the ancient Druid stone circle, the raven had already settled itself upon the tallest stone and started preening its feathers, seemingly unconcerned at the arrival of the Opal Knight and his companions. The site stood in the middle of a meadow, naturally protected by a circle of ancient trees. Centuries of wind and rain had worn down the huge, ancient stones, but, nonetheless, they still told their stories of what they had witnessed when the Druids' influence dominated ancient Irish culture.

The Druids controlled the elements—wind, water, fire, and earth. Their magic allowed them to shape-shift at will. Unlike lycanthropes, whom the moon influences during its cycles, Druids could shape-shift into any animal at will. During a Druid's ancient initiation rite, an animal chose him, and this connection remained unbroken in all aspects of both of their lives. The Druids lived in secrecy and practiced arcane arts. Contrary to what the Church wanted the people to believe, Druids lived good, genuine lives in perfect harmony with the world and nature. They knew how to mix plants, herbs, roots, and minerals to make poisons and with the same ingredients could provide the antidote. They studied magic and lived to provide for the good of the village they belonged, but so did their female counterparts—witches.

Like the Druids, witches lived good lives, not evil. Unlike the Druids, witches could not shape-shift. They could communicate with nature but not as well. Witches mixed potions like the Druids but also used incantations or spells to work their magic.

Both Druids and witches advocated love of every person, every animal, and the world in its entirety. They celebrated and oftentimes led the community festivals, such as Beltane and Samain. Beltane was considered one of the most important festivals, the Festival of Light of the Earth. This was a time of rebirth. Great tribal gatherings occurred on hilltops. Tribespeople extinguished fires in house fireplaces and relit them from the great bonfires built for the festivals. They also walked between the sacred bonfires for purification. The veil between the two worlds is thin at this time, allowing fairies to cross over. Samain was the largest and most important festival. The tribespeople prepared to confront the winter by relighting their house fires from the sacred bonfires. The possibility of death became prevalent during this time. Here also, because the veil between this world and the underworld was thin, ancestors were able to visit their descendants' households.

The social status of Druids and witches rose in prominence once they proved their worth and value to villages. Most villages and small towns had between two and five Druids living on the outskirts in small huts, where they communed with nature and animals. Stone circles became the central points of the Druids' power. Able to control and manipulate the conditions around them and their dwellings, Druids lived comfortably in the harshest of weather. They also had the inherent aptitude to read the elements and to give forewarning to villagers of approaching foul weather. Irish society at this time depended heavily on its agriculture. With the Druids' forewarning of dreadful weather, the villagers and farmers could protect their crops from the potential devastation that floods or hail brought.

The witches lived in the village proper. Because of their unique magical potions and spells, the villagers or townsfolk often sought out witches to heal their many ailments or injuries. Witches became valuable companions to the military, merchant vessels, and travelers. They fashioned charms and chanted protection spells for travelers against highwaymen; for merchant vessels, they did so to protect them against krakens and other assorted sea monsters of the deep ocean. These spells actually protected the creatures more than the sailors by concealing the creatures from the vessels and sailors, thus assuring that no harm befell the creatures. For the military, witches' charms enhanced the qualities of armor and weapons for soldiers, provided, of course, that they paid the right the price. These enhancements gave the soldier a significant advantage in battle.

Most payments for Druids were made in the form of protection, for which the Druids usually employed knights. Witches also required protection, but usually wanted rare ingredients for their spells and potions in addition. Very rarely did they ask for gold or platinum, and never silver.

The Opal Knight slowed as he approached the ancient

Druid ritual site, identifiable by the stone circle. Daniel reflected on many of the events he had witnessed there prior to becoming a knight. He stopped just short of the stone circle, recalling this circle as ancient sacred ground. A common misconception of many churchgoers was that the Druids used this place for evil rituals consisting of animal and child sacrifices to give the Druids their strength and power.

Most considered the Druids and witches to be evil and minions of Satan. As Church influence grew over the Irish, the local populace continued to misunderstand both Druids and witches as evil beings. The Church gained power and popularity, and it ensured that its rivals—in Ireland's case, Druids and witches—were ostracized by popularizing prejudice and hate. With its rivals eventually chased out, the Church became the sole benefactor of the people's attention. Daniel understood the Druid and witch way of life. As a young boy and, later, a young man, Daniel became educated in the arcane arts that the Druids and witches practiced. His path eventually led him to the Church. Daniel understood both, and this comprehension often caused him to straddle the two worlds. More often than not, the worlds were not in harmony, resulting in much distress. Daniel knew that neither the Druids nor the witches were evil. The Druids used the Mound to perform their rituals, and no one or thing could enter unless that person or thing claimed to be a Druid, witch, or protector.

While Macha and Balor remained beyond the perimeter, the raven flew onto the most worn stone of the circle, and Daniel entered.

Daniel walked slowly around the inside of the ancient

stone circle, reminiscing about the many rituals that had occurred there throughout his tenure as protector. He had witnessed rituals older than most religions. Balor and Macha assumed their usual protective positions, with Macha furthest out, grazing peacefully, and Balor keeping pace with his master within arm's reach. Both remained ever alert for any sign of trouble or danger. As Daniel neared each stone, he touched it. Sometimes he paused and smiled; other times he became sad and angry. He had always had the gift, but he never told anyone since the Church would have targeted him as a witch or some other creature hated by the Vatican. Whenever Daniel came into contact with old objects, such as relics, buildings, furniture, or natural objects such as trees or stones, they told Daniel what they had witnessed. These visions consisted of anything from battles to arguments even to animals' passing. Daniel did not have any control over when the visions came to him or what he saw when they did arrive. The visions occurred as memories to him. As memories, Daniel felt he had experienced each.

He continued his walk, touching each stone in the circle. Several times, he experienced a "memory." He recalled the Druids working with nature to predict the weather for a century. One memory even showed an attempt by the Church to destroy the circle hundreds of years ago. Somehow, the Church could not locate the circle even when the Church representatives appeared within steps of the stones. Another memory showed Cassandra's initiation into the witches' coven.

The memories of her became vivid, and he knew that they did not belong to him. Cassandra looked much older in these memories. At times, the memories caused Daniel much confusion. His love for her had brought him under suspicion from the Church many times—the same Church he had sworn a solemn oath to serve and protect. Daniel knew all those years ago that his destiny lay in protecting someone or something. As Daniel was a natural leader even as a child in the streets of Lough Inch, the other children seemed to flock to him and obey him as if they already knew him as a knight. Of course, his bravery set him apart from his peers and elders alike. He not only looked danger in the face, he sought it out.

About five years after his first meeting with Cassandra, young Daniel was running through the alleys of the town with several other children following. They sought some sort of adventure. In the distance, they heard the shouts of one of the vendors in the marketplace. Apparently, the vendor had failed to tether his horse, and it had gotten startled by some ravens flying about the village. Daniel and his followers heard the clipping and clopping of the horse getting closer and closer, until it became difficult to distinguish as clipping or clopping, combined with the sound of the wagon wheels rolling along the path. The combination of both and the *caw-caw* of the ravens overhead grew louder and louder. Almost everyone felt the tension of danger. Daniel pushed the other children behind him and peered around the edge of the alley. Across the street stood Cassandra. She had just placed her large tome on the bench. She had seen Daniel in the shadows, and she smiled and waved as she walked across her path to the wall. She exited her protective wall through the gate and looked behind her to ensure that her mother had not noticed her abandoning her studies. Seeing that Iliana was nowhere in sight, Cassandra skipped toward Daniel and the other children.

Daniel screamed and waved frantically for Cassandra to stay back, but she failed to understand the warning and continued her course. The horse and cart moved at an incredible speed. It would be impossible for it to stop in time. Without any thought, Daniel bolted out of the alley toward Cassandra with the horse and cart barreling down on Cassandra less than fifty yards away. She stopped, perplexed, as she watched Daniel run toward her, and then her gaze shifted left. She stood in horror as the horse became bigger and bigger. In the next moment, Cassandra had rolled over several times on the ground and come to a stop against the wall that protected her home.

To Daniel, everything moved at an incredibly slow pace. As he ran to Cassandra, he moved his head back and forth, extending his field of vision. Cassandra's smile slowly turned into a grimace of fear as she turned toward the danger. The horse's eyes seemed red with anger—very strange. Various trinkets flew off the cart, such as tin cups, plates, and a wooden birdcage with a brightly colored bird inside it. Daniel ran through a mud puddle and splashed dirty water up onto his clothing. Knowing the horse and cart would crush Cassandra within seconds, Daniel acted. He dove the rest of the distance toward Cassandra. As he wrapped his arms around her, the force lifted both of them into the air. Daniel spun in the air as he and Casandra cleared the path of the speeding horse and cart. Daniel landed with a thud with Casandra on top of him. They rolled until they came to a stop against the stone wall. The horse and cart continued for another hundred yards until both came to a halt.

Iliana heard the commotion and ran out of the cottage toward the heap of arms and legs. Daniel's followers and several villagers, including the vendor, arrived at the scene.

Daniel's friends surrounded and praised him.

"That was amazing, Daniel!"

"I thought Cassandra was dead, but you saved her!"

Daniel and Cassandra untangled themselves. Daniel had bruised his back and scraped his arms and legs, and he was bleeding from his forehead. Other than her light blue dress being torn at the hem, however, Cassandra was none the worse for wear. Iliana snatched up Cassandra and inspected her for injuries.

"Cassandra, how many times have I told you never to wander outside the wall?"

"All the time, every day, Mother, but …"

"But, nothing! I told you time and time again—close contact with them, especially this boy, would be the death of you."

"Yes, Mother, but …"

"Get in the house."

Cassandra held her head down during the berating from her mother and noticed her torn hem. She knelt down and tore the rest of the hem cleanly from its stitching. Daniel had sat up by then and shook the stars from his head. Cassandra moved to stand in front of Daniel.

"Daniel, you *are* my brave knight and protector."

Cassandra tied the torn hem gently around his right wrist, where Daniel wore it for several months until it frayed into threads. Then Cassandra replaced it with another, a custom the two maintained well into adulthood. Daniel stood and thanked Cassandra. She smiled and ran giggling into the house.

Iliana followed, but before she entered the gate, she beckoned Daniel to her. "Come here, boy!"

Daniel ran to her. Iliana bent so she was eye to eye with him and whispered something that only Daniel could hear. She stood upright, turned, and went through the gate, which slammed shut on its own. Then she disappeared into the cottage.

Daniel returned to the other children in the alley. In the shadows, Daniel leaned against one of the mossy walls that framed the alley.

"What did she say to you?" one of the children asked.

"Did she kill you?"

"No, she is going to eat him."

Daniel smiled as he admired the hem tied around his wrist. "None of those things, my friends. Obviously, I'm not dead or eaten."

"Then what did she tell you?"

"She told me to stay away from her daughter, to never see or speak to her again."

"That's why you are smiling?"

"No. She also said thank you."

Daniel loved these kinds of memories. He smiled and continued his walk, dragging his feet as if he still slogged through the mud until the memories wrested themselves from his mind. Something seemed to startle the raven. It cawed several times, and took to the air. Daniel felt lost and alone. He needed guidance and comfort. Daniel decided to seek the one place that always provided that guidance and comfort he sought.

"Let's go, my friends." Daniel and animal companions headed in the direction of the abbey.

The abbey was at the opposite end of the village, a location chosen for two specific reasons. The first was that it ensured that the representative of the Catholic Church stayed as far away from the heathen circle the ancients called the Mound. The second, which had a more practical application, was for defense. The abbey was a huge edifice, remarkable in that it withstood the many Viking raids even though many of the churches it oversaw fell to the plunder of the raiders. The path to the main entrance was along a curving, switchback, narrow road intentionally designed as such to discourage friends and enemy alike. It was too narrow for any substantial force to use. Horses could traverse the path only in single file, and depending on the weapons and armor, no more than three men across could walk it. It was barely worth attempting an attack knowing that the men could easily be picked off by archers from the high towers. Although built on a high hilltop similar to the Mound, the abbey was protected on the rear by a high, sheer cliff and on its two sides by steep, sloped, rugged terrain. The entire abbey was under the protection of local conscripts, their loyalty driven by their religious fervor and fanaticism.

Dusk crept up the hill toward the abbey from the village below. If Daniel wanted to get inside before nightfall, he would have to hurry since no one was admitted once the night took over. He mounted Macha to make the climb quicker, but as he made the last turn of the switchback path, he saw and heard the large wooden doors slam shut. Several bolts were pushed into place, followed by crossbars that exceeded the width of the doors and were dropped into place at intervals up the length of the doors.

Daniel's anxiety rose within his chest. He began to sweat profusely even though the air had a slight chill about it. His breathing came in short pants, much like Balor after a chase. Worst of all, the memories crept back into his mind. The dense cloud cover would certainly prevent any moonlight from pushing away the darkness. Daniel had to get inside; the fires there were many and large. He would feel safe only inside. He dismounted, ran to the huge portcullis, and pounded furiously. The sentries from the towers took aim with their bows as the sergeant of the guard from inside the gate made the usual query of those seeking entrance.

"Who goes there?"

"It is I, Sir Daniel, the Opal Knight. I seek an audience with the abbot."

By now, Macha and Balor had caught up with their master and flanked him on either side. The unexpected appearance of the three seemed ominous and dangerous to the tower archers. This was relayed by hand signals to the sergeant of the guard.

"No one gains entry once dusk settles."

"I must see him!" Daniel pounded again.

"Cease! Cease this at once!"

"It is not quite dusk. I have time," Daniel pleaded.

"Cease, sir, or I will be compelled to give my archers the order."

With this, the archers drew their bowstrings taut.

Another voice from inside addressed the sergeant of the guard. "You fool. That is Sir Daniel, the Opal Knight. Don't you know him?"

"Your eminence, I have my orders."

"Mind your station. He is our knight! Open the gate immediately," the familiar voice of the abbot demanded.

Daniel and his companions heard the huge iron bars slid back from their emplacement and the bolts drawn back to their locked positions. The huge doors creaked open. Just beyond the swing path of the doors stood a medium-height, slightly built man dressed in the long, brown, woolen habit of a monk. His feet were bare and his head completely bald. The bend at the shoulders was now permanent from many years of study in the abbey library, and his gnarled hands were clasped together at his waist as if in prayer.

"Quickly, my son, come in. Come in."

Daniel ran to the abbot and knelt in reverence on his right knee. Macha and Balor hesitantly entered, both ever wary when they entered the high walls of man.

Although the abbot did not physically touch Daniel, the knight sensed above his head the hands of the abbot. Daniel heard the abbot murmur a blessing. Daniel felt at peace even though he could not understand the prayer spoken in the Church language, Latin. The abbot raised Daniel by the right arm to his feet and embraced him.

"Come, Opal Knight. We will eat, drink, and talk about things."

"Father, I have questions—"

The abbot cut him off. "Relax, my son. There's plenty of time for questions, but you must take care of your basic needs first."

The abbot patted Daniel on the shoulder, turned, and headed toward the main hall of the abbey. The main hall doubled as the congregation hall and dining room, but it would be several minutes before the two sat and ate. Known for their love of nature, the monks of Lough Inch took great care of Daniel's companions. Macha was led to the stable to have her saddle and tack removed. She was given a good rubdown, watered, and fed with fresh hay and oats. She felt at ease with these men. They were very kind and loving. Balor, on the other hand, refused any handling. While he did not bite anyone, he eluded the monks who tried to collar and leash him. After several minutes of chasing the huge mastiff, the monks decided to just put down a bowl of water and scraps of meat for the dog. Balor ate and eventually sat near a wall with his back to it. He continued to sniff the air and twitched his ears, ever ready. Balor's keen eyes penetrated the darkness, seeking his master.

CHAPTER 4

From the village below, the abbey did not appear large. Under any weather conditions, the villagers could see the high walls and church tower of the abbey. However, inside the walls, the abbey contained a barracks for the sentries, stable, library, dining hall/congregation hall, living quarters for the twenty monks, kitchen, and brewery. Daniel followed the abbot down the damp, poorly lit halls. They walked past the living quarters, where they heard the whispers of the monks praying in private. The aromas from the kitchen wafted through the cracks of the heavy oak door. Smells of beef and lamb stew with a blend of carrots, potatoes, onions, and cabbage blended with the smell of fresh baked bread and filled the corridor. The scents danced under Daniel's nose and teased his stomach. Although distracted by the kitchen smells, Daniel's attention turned to what the abbot said to him about taking care of basic needs. At that moment, hunger topped the list of basic needs, and Daniel could not wait until they sat and ate. It seemed like weeks since had eaten indoors, away from the dark and cold. As they entered the dining hall, the abbot gestured for Daniel to sit next to him. Two monks immediately brought in a flask of wine, cups, and a loaf of bread still steaming from the oven. Abbey tradition dictated that the responsibility for serving guests fell to the two monks presently under a vow of silence. Both monks wore similar garb as the abbot's. Theirs, however, had a more ragged appearance. They fashioned their hair in the stereotypical monk fashion, with locks uniformly cut in length around the entire head with the very central top of the head shaved bald.

Daniel opened his mouth to speak, but the abbot lifted his right forefinger to his lips and gave the blessing. Daniel held his question as the abbot took the warm loaf in his hands, broke off one end, and handed it to Daniel. Daniel took the piece and began to eat. Between bites, he sipped his wine. Both tasted good and sated him, and he relaxed. The abbot also ate and drank while he watched Daniel. When Daniel made eye contact, the abbot nodded.

"Father, what did you mean by saying that basic needs had to be met before questions could be answered?"

"Ah. Daniel, man has two basic needs that must be met before he can make good, sound decisions, one of which you are taking care of right now—hunger, by eating this beautiful bounty the Lord has provided. The other is feeling safe and secure. Once these basic needs are met, then one may delve deeper into his heart, mind, and soul. He seeks to gain control of three primal emotions that causes his mind and heart to wander. Wandering causes one to make unsound decisions based on those primal needs or emotions. Those three primal emotions are anger, loneliness, and exhaustion."

"But, Father, I have made decisions my entire life while hungry, angry, lonely, tired, or unsafe. I have experienced all of them at once and still made sound decisions."

"Yes, that's true, and certainly it is the nature of your profession, my knight, but you are not trying to defeat an enemy of the Church right now, are you? No. You are not. You are angry. You feel lost and alone. You are exhausted mentally, physically, and spiritually. You feel as if everyone is your enemy. Because of all of the primal emotions surfacing at once, you feel confused. This confusion will cause you to make an unsound and, possibly, dangerous decision either for yourself or for one about whom you care deeply."

"That's possible, Father," Daniel conceded. "I do feel as if everywhere I turn, I am confronted by an enemy, but how do you know?"

"Because you have the same look of torment you had when you first sought me out," the abbot revealed.

Daniel thought back to that one time that concerned his training. From age twelve to sixteen, a hermit had mentored Daniel. This hermit dwelt in the forest outside of Lough Inch. No one remembered the hermit's name, but everyone knew him to be very skilled in many arts. Every few years, the hermit took a young man under his instruction. By the time Daniel turned sixteen, he had become an expert in all of the hermit's arts. The hermit recommended that Daniel leave Lough Inch to pursue more training and experience the world. Daniel felt he could not leave Cassandra, but he felt a tug from deep inside his mind and heart calling him to a greater good. Daniel climbed the switchback trail to the abbey and sought an audience with the abbot.

"How can I help you?" the abbot had asked.

"Father, I do not know what to do."

The abbot sat with the young man and prayed. After several hours, Daniel felt a great burden lifted from his shoulders as he had made his decision.

The abbot explained, "The Spirit of God removed that burden. He cleared your mind, heart, and spirit. It was not until the Holy Spirit intervened that were you able to make this decision."

Daniel had thanked the abbot and left Lough Inch to pursue the greater good—to continue his training to become a knight.

"So tell me, Sir Knight," the abbot began with a grin, "what is troubling you now? Why seek out the Church?"

"Father, do you know of Cassandra?"

"Yes, I do. If I am not mistaken, she has been accused of witchcraft by some unscrupulous sorts—"

Daniel interrupted, "She is not evil!"

"If you'll let me finish—accused of witchcraft, but no evidence of such was ever brought to my or the Church's attention."

"Yes. I apologize for my outburst. You must also be aware that I have known Cassandra since we were both children. During all that time, we have grown to love each other."

"Of course, Daniel. Cassandra is the one who named you Opal Knight. If not for her, you never would have been shown your path of becoming a Knight of the Church. Does Cassandra have something to do with your troubles?"

"Yes, Father, she does. A few days ago there was a fire …"

The abbot blessed himself. "Terrible. So terrible. I did not hear of any loss. Wait. Daniel, do you mean that the fire was in Cassandra's cottage?"

Daniel could only nod.

"My son, I am so sorry. Are you seeking me to preside over the funeral?"

Daniel's mind began to wander. He realized he was getting angry again. "Funeral? There's no body."

"What? What did you say?"

"There's no body. Her cottage was razed to the ground. Cassandra is gone."

"What do you mean 'no body'? No one could live through that."

"Father, that's why I sought you out."

The abbot composed himself. "Daniel, together we have taken care of most, but not all, of your basic, primal emotions. You still feel angry. Prayer and rest will calm you. It is time for you to rest, and I will pray for your soul."

The abbot raised his left hand, and the two monks hurried into the hall.

"Show our brave knight to the guest quarters. Guard over him."

The abbot rose and disappeared through an archway on the opposite side where he and Daniel had entered an hour earlier. Daniel rose to follow, but each monk took him by an elbow and led him away.

The two monks led Daniel to the opposite end of the living quarters, away from the other monks' quarters. He thought about asking the two monks some further questions that the abbot had evaded, but he thought better of it since neither would speak anyway. The monks stopped at the end of a corridor where a lone room awaited with its door open. Daniel stepped inside and looked around in the darkness. After the monks lit two candles in the room, Daniel surveyed the layout of his quarters.

The room was humble, just like all the other monks' quarters. A cot with straw bedding was pushed against one wall. A single wool blanket, slightly frayed and worn, had been folded at the foot of the bed, and the head was near the open window. It faced east so that the light and warmth from the sunrise would wake him. A table and chair were placed under the window. On the bed rested the Holy Bible. The gray, stone walls were as bare as the floor. The two candles produced the only available light in the evening, and a chamber pot completed the decor. Daniel took notice that the room was not damp, which was rather strange considering they were in middle of the rainy season. Although his host was exceedingly gracious and the two monks cordial, Daniel still felt like a prisoner. He sat on the bed and said good night to the monks.

They bowed slightly as they backed out of the room. Daniel heard the door being locked from the outside. If he had not known that it was common practice for all monks to be locked in their rooms after nightfall, Daniel would have certainly surmised that he was being held prisoner. He scrutinized his surroundings more carefully. Seeing nothing out of the ordinary, he stood up and began to pace. His thoughts were frantic. He sat back down, and his hand touched the Bible. Daniel smiled for the first time in days.

"He always knows when I need Him most," he said aloud.

Daniel randomly flipped through the pages of the book. When he stopped, he read,

> My soul faints for Your salvation, but I hope in Your word. My eyes fail from searching for Your word saying, "When will You comfort me?" For I have become like a wineskin in smoke yet I do not forget Your statutes. How many are the days of Your servant? When will you execute judgment on those who persecute me? The proud have dug pits for me, which is not according to Your law. All Your commandments are faithful, they persecute me wrongfully; help

me! They almost made an end of me on
earth, but I did not forsake Your precepts.
Revive me according to Your loving
kindness, so that I may keep the testimony
of Your mouth. (Psalm 119:81–88)

As Daniel finished, he felt relieved. He lay on the bed of
straw and soon drifted off to sleep. As he slept, he dreamt.
Daniel's dreams always seemed so vivid not only in sound
but also in colors, smells, and tastes. All of his senses were
heightened.

He walked along the village path toward the church.
Many of the villagers greeted him as they had often done.
They were grateful to him for the many deeds he had
performed. Daniel remained humble. The path grew steeper
and steeper, and it became more of a struggle to get to the
church steps. But he had to get there. Something pulled him
toward the church. It wasn't Sunday or a holy day when he
had to attend mass, but something urged him to get inside.
The answer was there. Answer to what? The closer he got,
the steeper the path became and the farther away the church
seemed to move. Daniel felt frustrated and angry. As he
walked, Daniel recalled his training. He closed his eyes and
thought of peace; he thought of Cassandra. The more he
thought of Cassandra's smile, laugh, and walk, the easier the
path became to navigate. Daniel opened his eyes. He saw
the church within reach. He climbed the three wooden steps
and pushed open the two large, wooden doors. The doors
appeared similar to those that protected the abbey. Daniel

entered as he had many times before. He had always enjoyed this part since he was a young boy because, as he entered, Daniel imagined the beautiful stained-glass windows of various colors greeting him. When the sun shone through the windows, the colors and images became even more beautiful. The images appeared lifelike and often seemed to move, as if telling the admirer their stories. Saint Patrick garbed in his green robe and holding his staff drove out the snakes. The snakes slithered along the ground defeated. Saint Daniel lay among the lions, completely tame and docile, purring as Daniel stroked each one as if it were a pet kitten. Saint Francis, dressed the same as the monks who honored his name, stood among many forest animals, speaking to them in a language only the animals could understand.

But the stained-glass windows in Daniel's dream differed. Instead of Saint Patrick, there was a knight on horseback with a dog running alongside. An ugly hag over a boiling cauldron of murky gruel filled the space held by Saint Daniel. The third did not depict Saint Francis but a man and woman embracing each other. As Daniel looked in wonder from one stained-glass window to another, the images came alive. The lone mounted knight suddenly turned his back, the hag's cauldron boiled over, and she cackled in evil laughter. The embraced lovers, however, kept their embrace. Daniel approached the stained-glass lovers and saw that they were Cassandra and himself. They embraced and stared into each other's eyes. Daniel stared into the dark, brown eyes with speckled purple and yellow; Cassandra gazed up into Daniel's green eyes, which seemed to change color depending on his mood. As he neared, something happened. The embrace was violently interrupted by a loud explosion, and the stained-glass window blew apart. Shards of colored glass flew across the church proper. Daniel stood as sharp pieces sprayed passed him. Some embedded into the wooden pews and stone walls. One shard that contained Cassandra's eye found its way to the feet of Daniel. The eye wept. He looked up at the empty frame in shock. As he absorbed the horror of the empty frame, Daniel observed that one lone piece of stained glass dangled precariously by its lead frame. It contained Daniel's and Cassandra's intertwined fingers.

Daniel woke and reached out. As he opened his eyes, he felt the warmth of the sun on his face. He realized he had been having a dream, or a nightmare. Daniel jumped off the cot, and the Bible that was resting on his chest fell to the floor and opened to a very different chapter and verse: "But take heed to yourselves lest your hearts be weighed down with carousing, drunkenness, and cares of this life" (Luke 21:34).

Daniel had found his faith late in life compared to the rest of the citizens of his town and country. He knew that his God worked mysteriously but always spoke to His humble servants. The previous night, when God had first intervened, Daniel realized that the psalm was intended to help relieve him of his adversity. However, this last passage about drunkenness and carousing did not seem to make any sense to Daniel. Why would the book open to this passage? Why would Daniel be reminded of a very dark time of his life when he had been lost? He had already made his penance for those sins. Why would he be shown a path back to a place where he had spent so many days drinking and carousing?

"Of course," Daniel whispered.

Daniel gently shook his head and smiled to himself. He clasped his hands in front of his waist, closed his eyes, lifted his chin, and prayed aloud. As he ended his prayer, he heard the metallic click of the lock opening. Daniel opened the door and stepped out into the dank corridor. The abbey corridors hummed with the monks heading toward the chapel for morning mass. Daniel joined but kept his thoughts to himself and maintained a reverent posture. He could not remember the last time he had attended mass in the abbey. As Daniel and the monks neared the chapel, he noticed a small contingent of soldiers standing outside the doors as if at the ready. The monks hesitated in the procession toward the chapel, so Daniel knew that the presence of the soldiers was not normal.

The monks' hesitance made Daniel's vigilance and training take over. He proceeded to make his way toward the edge of the slow-moving throng. If the soldiers' presence made the monks nervous, then Daniel could be the only reason they were there. The soldiers were looking for him. It seemed somewhat strange since the soldiers could have taken him from his room at any time during the night, he thought. But an arrest of a knight would have aroused the sleeping monks and raised suspicion. No, his arrest would have to be made public and under the ruse of some trumped-up charge. The soldiers would make some move or say something to bring Daniel's temper to the surface, thus causing him to look like a maniac.

The Opal Knight had been in this type of situation many times before. Daniel quickly surveyed his surroundings and recalled the layout of the abbey. Several smaller corridors branched off the main corridor. He attempted to continue moving toward the outside of the moving mass of monks without drawing suspicion. He bowed his head ever so slightly to give the appearance of prayerful meditation while at the same time keeping his eyes raised to watch the soldiers.

The abbot craned his neck to gain a better view of the approaching monks; he especially looked for Daniel in order to warn the guards of his approach. It was not difficult to locate the knight. Daniel dressed differently, stood taller, and occupied more space than the humble monks he attempted to hide among. The abbot raised his right hand and pointed toward the Opal Knight. Seeing this, Daniel stepped to the corridor on his left, and once out of sight, he picked up his pace. Although he believed he was in danger, he did not wish to fight or, worse, take a life on sacred, consecrated ground. As Daniel moved, he tried each door in hopes that he could enter a room and hide. He needed to escape, but leaving the abbey in daylight without raising an alarm would be extremely difficult. Besides, he could not leave Macha and Balor behind.

Daniel found an open door and entered. He slid the dead bolt slowly into place. As he turned, he was greeted by hundreds of tomes in the library. The room was magnificent—not magnificent in the sense of paintings and tapestries but because of its shelves and shelves of books. Daniel loved to read and was fluent in many languages. In his training, he had traveled to many lands and quickly learned how to speak, write, and read in not only many country's languages but also in the regional dialects. Monks worked at several tables every day, transcribing and studying the books of the library.

CHAPTER 5

Daniel's vision soon adapted to the dimly lit library. He had some time before the quiet library would become busy with the scholarly activity of the monks. They had Mass first and then breakfast before attending to their studies and writing. The guards would search for him throughout the abbey, expecting him to escape as soon as possible. The sergeant of the guard, not expecting the Opal Knight to linger about, had doubled the number of sentries at all possible exits. As Daniel walked through the stacks of books, he decided to make his way to the stack farthest away from the entrance to hide until nightfall. As he walked through the aisles, he noticed many books he had read and others he did not recognize. Naturally, a majority of the books in the library had a theological theme. Writings from Saint Augustine and Saint Thomas Aquinas filled the writing tables of the scribes, as well as the Bible. Additionally, many books and scrolls that referenced the ancient Greek and Roman Empires filled numerous shelves. Daniel became curious as to why an abbey library held material that was contradictory to the Church's teachings and, obviously, heretical in nature. Daniel would have plenty of time to ponder this newfound knowledge as he found a dark, secluded corner. A labyrinth of shelves upstairs and away from the soon-to-be-busy book depository protected his hidden position. He hunkered down and rested but kept alert and vigilant for any approaching footsteps.

The door to the library opened. Daniel remained on edge only for a short period of time before he realized that the footsteps belonged to the scribes entering for their daily work. The monks lit many candles as they entered, and soon the library was bright enough to begin their research and transcription of the books. They began their work, and halfway through the morning, four guards entered to conduct a courtesy walk-through. As with any guard force or group of soldiers, unsupervised by their sergeant or knight, they just wanted to get the task done quickly and return to the barracks for some rest or gambling. Midday arrived, and the monks headed to the dining hall in a very orderly manner for noon prayers. Daniel maintained his position even though he had started to cramp a little, and he maintained his silence. After an hour, the monks returned and continued their work.

The day was relatively uneventful except for near the end of the day when the librarian made his usual rounds to ensure nothing was out of place. This was more a personally satisfying walk through the stacks than an actual security walkabout. Daniel heard the librarian shuffle toward him with a noticeable limp on his left side. The librarian neared the last stack in the rear of the alcove. The knight worried that he may have caused some books to be out of place, some subtle flaw that only the librarian would notice, and if the librarian corrected the mistake, he would discover Daniel. As the librarian drew closer, he suddenly turned and moved as quickly as his limp would permit toward some commotion in the yard. Daniel could not hear every word that was being yelled from the courtyard, but what he could decipher was, "The knight's horse and dog are vicious animals and will soon be sold.… That dog should be run through. He's mad …"

Daniel then heard the voice of the sergeant of the guard, "Neither horse nor dog will be mistreated. That is the order of the abbot." Upon hearing this, Daniel settled back into his resting position, relieved that his friends remained safe for the time being. He would not attempt to leave until after midnight.

The midnight call of the guard woke Daniel. He sipped some water, crawled from his hiding position, stood, and stretched to get the blood moving and loosen his cramped muscles. Daniel moved swiftly to the library door, crouched, and listened for any movement. He heard no discernable sound, so he cracked the door and stepped out. Daniel located a window that faced away from the guard towers. He stepped out onto the ledge and stealthily walked along the rooftops, making his way to the unlit side of the abbey. He climbed down onto the stable roof without making any sound, but the horses stirred from his scent. Daniel rolled off the stable roof and silently landed on his feet. Macha stepped out of the shadows. She was tied by her head harness to either sidewall of her stall. Although dirty, she looked well fed and had definitely not been harmed in any way.

Until Daniel could think through the circumstances, he could not trust anyone. However, he was encouraged that the guards and abbot still viewed all animals as creatures of God and treated them as such. Daniel led Macha out of her stall and saddled her. She instinctively knew to remain quiet but could not resist nuzzling her friend's neck. The knight had no idea where Balor was being held. He whispered his request to Macha, and she led the way to where the monks boarded Balor. As they approached, Daniel heard a low growl that stopped as the breeze shifted and Balor recognized his friends' scents. Daniel opened the cage door, and Balor stepped out. Daniel realized that this was the easy part. The difficult part of their escape was about to come.

Daniel would try his best not to kill anyone, but he could not promise himself no one would get injured.

The three united friends quickly greeted one another. Although they had spent only a day and night apart, it felt as if it had been years. The three had fought many battles together and worked instinctively well together. When in battle, Daniel was always in command of the other two, and they waited for his voice, whistle, or hand commands. Daniel relied heavily on Macha's and Balor's senses when visibility became limited. The three navigated through the shadows. The sentry torches faced out, giving them visibility on the approach of weary travelers, friends, or potential danger. All threats were presumed to approach from outside the abbey; therefore, the sentries always faced out. Nevertheless, Balor led the way in the shadows using his sense of smell to guide them, Daniel walked in the middle to quickly respond to any threat from front or rear, and Macha took the rear using her extraordinary sense of hearing to protect them from any surprise attack from behind.

Twice, Balor's keen sense of smell prevented an altercation. Both times, Balor smelled the approach of guards with enough time for the three to freeze in the shadows and let them pass. The primary concern was how to get through the front gate. The moon was high and bright. Daniel grew worried as he huddled in the shadows thinking of a way out. He had to get his friends and himself out, and he was still confused as to what was happening and why the abbot wanted him arrested. Instinctively, he knew he could not risk a trial. He was so confused, but Daniel's Creator watched over him. The moonlight began to fade as thick, dark clouds quickly moved in. Daniel knew he had made the right decision. The sky opened up, and a torrential rain accompanied by a strong wind began to pummel the countryside. Daniel's military background assured him that the guards at the walls and gate would seek shelter in some alcove, thus giving him and his companions the ability to move closer. The wind and rain allowed for the companions to move less stealthily, and shortly the three neared the bunker where various weapons were kept.

Balor sniffed the air and sat down, indicating to Daniel that no one was around the corner. Daniel took a quick peek. He gave Balor and Macha the signal to stay and wait for his command to follow, stay, or attack. Daniel covered the distance between where they hid and the gate in several seconds. As he approached, a guard stepped out of the shadows, drew his sword, and challenged.

"Ha—." The guard was cut off by a small stone thrown with incredible accuracy to his throat. The guard struggled to breathe but still lived. He was more concerned with his difficulty in breathing than with what Daniel was doing. Unable to ward off the punch to his solar plexus, the guard collapsed. Without a break in stride, the Opal Knight ran to the gate and, as silently as possible, lifted the metal bar off the gate. Daniel whistled; Balor and Macha moved from the shadows and trotted toward him. Daniel opened the gate, but it creaked and moaned as he pushed his huge frame against it.

"Damn rusty hinges," Daniel muttered.

The sentries on the wall peered out of their shelter and hollered, "Halt! Halt!"

Daniel looked up and noticed that one had notched an arrow into his short bow. Daniel drew his dagger and let it fly. It hit the archer in his drawing shoulder, and he released the arrow. The shaft whistled through the air and buried itself into the gate inches above Daniel's head. Had Daniel waited a split second, he would have been minus one eye. He leaped onto Macha's back and, with Balor alongside, burst through the open gate and headed down the switchback road. The rain got heavier and the torches dimmed, making it very difficult for the sentries to find their target. Daniel heard commands, but there was no pursuit. The abbey sentries had no jurisdiction in Lough Inch.

Daniel, Macha, and Balor ran until they got to the bottom of the hill and entered the village, which was dark and muddy from the rain. Daniel knew where he had to go to start getting answers—the Dancing Giant, the village tavern, where most of the men visited at least once a week and their wives visited at least once a week to retrieve them. The tavern had served as a brothel before the church established its power and now acted as a temporary boarding house for travelers, sailors, and anyone who sought anonymity.

Daniel steered Macha toward his destination. When they arrived, he walked past the tavern and around the back to ensure they had not been followed. Once satisfied, he left Balor and Macha under cover at the stable where there was plenty of straw for warmth and a trough for water. To the confusion of his friends, Daniel walked in the opposite direction of the tavern, made a left, and then made another. He walked completely exposed to the torrent. Daniel wanted the patrons and keepers to believe he had arrived on foot after a long journey and could not play that part well if he was not soaked through and muddied up and down his body.

Daniel walked around the edge of the village so his approach would be opposite from the road leading to the abbey. He slogged through the muddy road leading into town, passing several shops that were closed for the night and many cottages. Some were dark and some lit by lone candles. Every now and then, he heard the cry of a baby probably looking for its midnight feeding. Several dogs barked in warning as he wandered too near their territory. The downpour tapered off as Daniel approached the center of the town. How quickly circumstances change. Just a few days earlier, he had ridden in as a hero to save his Cassandra, and now he was a fugitive from the church he served and loved. Daniel was still confused. He picked up his pace toward the tavern. He had to get answers.

It was well after midnight, and as the knight approached, he heard the din of the tavern. Steins and mugs clinking, singing, carousing, and laughter broke the silence of the village. Although the tavern catered mostly to travelers, several locals still frequented the inn daily. Daniel needed to remain incognito. He stepped into the shadows of a doorway and recalled his training. A man as large as himself had to alter everything to avoid recognition. He loosened his wet, muddy, worn cloak and slumped his shoulders so he would not appear as tall. His hair was matted against his face, obstructing some of his features, and he pulled the hood low over his eyes. To complete the deception, he continued to muddy his entire body and clothing and altered his stride. Daniel now walked more deliberately and with a noticeable limp.

As Daniel reached to open the large wooden door, it swung open and he witnessed a man as tall and stout as he was being tossed out by the peacekeeper. The peacekeeper was a Goliath. He stood easily seven feet tall and weighed more than three hundred pounds. His job was what his title related—keeping the peace in the tavern. If any argument broke out or even a sudden fight, the peacekeeper would immediately throw the guilty parties out, and never through the door or windows. That's why the owner had a door guard. His job was to protect the door from being broken. The door guard had to remain alert and ready to quickly push the door open when the peacekeeper was in the process of securing the peace.

Daniel entered the tavern, and the door guard closed the door behind him. The Goliath looked at Daniel. The knight's plan had the affect he required. No one recognized him. Daniel's appearance was one of a lone traveler. He was soaked to the bone, muddied from head to foot, and shivering. The peacekeeper leaned in close to Daniel and growled, "No trouble!"

Daniel leaned back away from the yellow-toothed grimace. "Not from me, kind sir. I just require a warm fire, a drink, and a meal."

"*Harrumph*. See that is all."

As Daniel walked away from the giant, the patrons returned to their distractions. Daniel made his way to the fireplace, which dominated the room. While he rubbed his hands together getting warm, he stood and faced the fire at an angle so he could watch the room out of the corner of his right eye. As his wet clothes dried and steamed, he took in the room. The proprietor, cook, and servers worked and lived in modest accommodations attached to the tavern. The tavern proper was fairly large. Long wooden tables and chairs were spread throughout, and the counter cornered off the back wall where the proprietor served the drinks and meals. In the back, a cook prepared simple meals for weary travelers. Three women aged between twenty and fifty years of age served the patrons. The eldest had also been a "server" when the tavern doubled as a brothel before the Church took control of the village. The Church influenced the local king to announce brothels as evil, decadent, and criminal. However, this was not to say that there were not still shenanigans going on in the back rooms.

Daniel peered around the room. It could hold fifty or sixty comfortably. Depending on the time of year and what holiday was being celebrated, perhaps up to 100 would fill the tavern. Tonight, no more than fifteen sat at the tables. The patrons themselves were most diverse. There were sailors, merchants, soldiers, mercenaries, and the usual villagers. A unique combination of loud and subdued groups and loners made this the perfect place to hear rumors from abroad and locally. Most rumors had some semblance of the truth to them.

The sailors and soldiers were dressed in their country of origin. Others bore the mark of the Church of Rome. The origins of the merchants and mercenaries were a little bit more difficult to distinguish, but not so for Daniel. The expert linguist, Daniel discovered each man's birthplace by his accent. The sailors and soldiers numbered five, three merchants, four mercenaries, and three locals rounded out the room.

The sailors and soldiers sat across from each other, challenging each other in drinking games and feats of strength, the only true winner being the proprietor. The locals sat together. They ate bowls of stew and broth, and drank mugs of mead. This table would provide the perfect source of local news. The merchants sat together at a table between the military and locals. Each listened for an opening to sell their wares. The mercenaries spread throughout the room, and tried to remain inconspicuous. It was important that Daniel played his role to perfection, the immediate threat being the four mercenaries.

Mercenaries were a very common sight in Lough Inch. With no declared war or Crusade, mercenaries constantly looked for some type of employment, sometimes as castle guards, constabulary forces, or even hunting down highwaymen. Daniel felt strange viewing the mercenaries as a threat, but his years of training and experience had taught him to trust his instincts. Daniel hailed the locals and limped toward an open chair as if he was the missing comrade.

The locals were noticeably drunk. The one facing Daniel waved back and then leaned in to his fellows to ask if either knew the stranger who seemed to know him. The mercenaries took some interest. Daniel approached and sat down with the villagers.

The youngest server quickly came over. "What would you like, sir?"

Daniel finished shaking hands with his friends and looked the server up and down. "You will do nicely." The wary locals guffawed and slapped their friend on the back. The server rolled her eyes. "Perhaps later."

Daniel smiled and raised his eyebrows. "What kind of stew do you have?"

"Gray."

"Hmm, I was unaware that gray was meat. Okay, I'll have a large bowl, and bring some mead for all of us."

The three locals' doubts about knowing Daniel quickly melted away when the server brought the round of drinks.

"So tell us, my friend, where are you coming from and where are you headed?"

"Roderick, can we at least get the stranger's name first, before we pry into his personal life?"

The three locals should have easily recognized him, but the dimly lit room, his beaten appearance, and his slow, slurred speech kept his secret safe. Of course, the fact that the three were heading into their fourth hour of steady drinking certainly helped.

"I am called Michael O'Farrell from Cork. I am a traveler seeking a new life in Galway."

"Hmm," Roderick began loudly, "Cork is a very similar city as Galway except on the south coast. Why leave it? Doesn't seem right."

Roderick's loud observation drew the attention of the mercenaries throughout the room. Without any thought, Michael (Daniel) responded, "I'm sorry, friend. I did not mean to deceive you, but you are right, I am hiding a secret."

One mercenary stood up.

Michael continued, "I was caught in the sleeping chambers of the Cork Gardia. So if I didn't leave Cork, there was a good chance I would have been in the bottom of the bay feeding the fish."

With this explanation, the locals guffawed and slapped their new hero on the back, just as the stew and mead arrived. They took this as an invitation to tell their own tales, some true, most exaggerated, of their own exploits with women throughout their travels. This continued about another hour and two more rounds.

Daniel laughed and shared some tales of his own—none of his true adventures, since those would certainly give away his identity. The tales Daniel did tell were boring and usually ended with him waking up with someone or somewhere he never expected. The mercenaries, with a discreet head nod from their leader, got up one by one and left the tavern. The leader left last. Daniel's ruse had worked, and then he could focus on trying to get some information. Daniel listened to some more tales and felt his opportunity to ask some seemingly innocent questions would come soon.

CHAPTER 6

The night moved toward early morning. The tavern filled and emptied several times before the keeper gave the nod to the servers that closing time neared. They stopped serving and started to clean up. The locals with whom Daniel sat tried to grab a server and negotiate a price. All were promptly slapped. The peacekeeper approached but was intercepted by Daniel.

"Sir, we were just leaving."

"*Harrumph*. Get them out now, or I will have to make sure they remember this night."

Daniel turned to his table mates. "My friends, this fine gentleman has politely recommended that we take our leave. I could not agree more."

Daniel staggered toward the peacekeeper just in case he needed to flex his muscles as the locals made for the exit. The locals still laughed and held onto one another as Daniel exited behind them.

"Well, friend," one of them said, "we are off to our castles to hear the wives complain about us being out late. Farewell."

Daniel had not finished gathering information, so he pressed them. "Wait. You are going to leave a stranger to these parts alone without any place to sleep?"

"Friend, go back inside and talk to the innkeeper. He will give you a bed in the back and, for a little more coin, some company." The villagers all laughed.

"I am looking for more respectable lodgings."

"What!" the villagers exclaimed, insulted.

"I'm sorry, friends," Daniel explained. "What I meant is I really need to sleep without any interruption."

"Hey, how about he stay with you, Brian?" one of the villagers suggested.

"I dunno. The wife might not like it."

"Brian, she's a good woman. She won't turn out a stranger."

"Yeah," another jumped in, "and besides, she won't try to kill you with a witness present." The other two snickered.

Brian thought a moment and then replied, "Friend, you are coming home with me."

All four said their good-byes, and Daniel and Brian headed away from the other two. This could not have worked out any better for Daniel. The villager who volunteered to house him for the night was the most talkative, and since they would walk past the rubble, extracting information from him would be easy for Daniel.

The two staggered down the street toward Brian's home, taking turns falling down and helping the other up. Village constables occasionally walked by and ordered the two to keep quiet and get home. They continued their chat as they made their way to the villager's cottage. Several times Daniel had to assist Brian when he staggered into some hedges. Brian had to help Daniel only once. This happened after Brian initiated Daniel into the Bush Guild, which consisted solely of Brian pushing him into a stand of thick, thorny bushes. They neared the site of the blaze.

"We will soon be passing the Opal Knight's cottage," Brian offered.

"What happened there?"

"It was terrible. The Opal Knight's house burnt to the ground while he was away on a mission for the Church."

"Who is the Opal Knight? Never heard of him."

"Really? If he wasn't real, he would be a legend."

"Well, I'm from the other side, so maybe his legend has not spread as far."

"Ridiculous! The Opal Knight is a hero. He was a hero before he was even a knight. You must have been away. Everyone has heard about him."

"Perhaps."

"I'm somewhat older, so I watched him grow up. He was not what you would expect of a future knight, that's for sure."

"Oh, a troublemaker or something like that?"

Daniel laughed courteously, but as he was going to ask more about the legend of the Opal Knight, the two turned on the path. There at the bend in the road was the remains of the fire. Daniel's anger stirred, but he controlled himself.

"What happened here?"

"Oh, my friend, it was tragic. Do you know that Opal Knight I was just talking about?"

"Certainly."

"This was his place. Or better, *their* place."

"Their?"

"Yes, he lived here with his bride. There were a lot of rumors that she was a witch, but he being a Knight of the Church, he would never be permitted to marry a witch, nor be a consort of one. At least not without penalties."

The remains still smoldered, and smoke rose in billows as the rain had poured down on the hot ashes. Daniel had to ask the hard questions—not for Brian, but for himself.

"Did anyone get hurt? Who did this? Why?"

Brian staggered as they approached the remains of the cottage. They stood quietly and stared in disbelief. Daniel felt the anger and pain swell inside his heart. A single, warm tear emerged from the corner of his left eye and made its way down the crease where his nose and cheek met. It dropped to the ground, and Daniel shook his head ever so slightly to regain his composure.

Brian stared into the smoldering rubble and answered, "My friend, it is believed that someone did die, but no body was found. There are various rumors of who is responsible and why. It's a terrible tragedy. Rumors had it that she was a witch. But I don't ever recall her kidnapping children, casting spells, or seeing her worship the devil."

Daniel's emotions got the best of him as he muttered, "Witches do not do that!"

"Huh? What?"

"Nothing. I didn't say anything."

"Hmm, thought I heard you say something. Anyway, it's difficult to believe she was a witch since the Opal Knight loved her and married her."

The rain came down heavily again, and the companions huddled deep within their cloaks. With the rain came a wind from the sea, chilling them to the bone. They both shivered, turned away from the devastation, and sloshed through the muddy street toward Brian's cottage. Daniel still had a couple of questions that needed answering, and he was not about to let his sole source of intelligence get away. As the two approached the cottage, Brian put one finger to his lips, dropped it, and ran it across his throat. Daniel surmised that if they made a lot of noise entering the humble abode, Brian may become the victim of his angry wife. Daniel's steps became much more stealthy, but Brian stumbled and kicked a bucket used to draw water from one of the wells scattered throughout the village. The bucket banged into the front door of the cottage with a loud crash that echoed up and down the nearby streets. Brian winced as if in terrible pain. Daniel moved to assist his injured friend, but Brian waved him off. The wince was in anticipation of what would happen next.

"Who's there?"

"Shh, I told you not to make any noise," Brian whispered and gestured as he turned to face Daniel.

"But I didn't—" Daniel was cut off.

"You good-for-nothing, no-good, evil man," a voice bellowed as the door opened.

A thin woman slightly taller than Brian stepped through the doorway out of the shadows. Her red hair was pulled back by a light, brown kerchief, revealing her light blue eyes, thin lips, and freckled face. Her dress was plain and patched in places but had originally been brown. Since she most likely was awoken from a deep sleep, she was barefoot. In her right hand was a candle, and as she pushed open the door, it was apparent by the look on her face and the tone of her voice that Brian had been guilty of coming home drunk quite often.

"Brian, you will to go to hell if you keep this up. The Good Lord will strike you down and send you straight to hell!"

"Ann, please don't bring the Lord into this. He don't mind that I go out with the lads, have some courage and a little of the craic."

"Brian, I think I should—" Daniel began.

"And who is this?" Ann interrupted. "Another one of your drunken cronies?"

"No, miss, I am actually—"

"Shut up! Keeping my husband out all hours of the night. He has a family to support, you know. A wife and three children who need that money he spent on you! You, get in the house." Ann pointed at Brian with the candle and dragged it through the air, showing him the way into the cottage.

The loud arguing woke their neighbors. Candles in windows up and down the street were lit. What started out as heading in the right direction for Daniel had suddenly made a turn for the worse. The last thing he wanted was attention.

Daniel decided it would be best to separate himself from the family quarrel that ensued from inside the cottage. He made his way back down the path. Since Brian was now occupied with perhaps saving his own life, Daniel needed to seek answers elsewhere. He needed to look through the rubble of his cottage. There had to be something that could tell him what happened to Cassandra. He had little time as dawn approached. Daniel picked up his pace and soon was at the site of the fire.

The smoke quickly dissipated to only some wisps of gray slowly reaching up toward heaven like outstretched fingers in one last gasp to be pulled to safety. Daniel recollected the moment he had first seen the remains. He was no longer ashamed or fearful. This emotion was something he had not felt in a very long time. Anger had kept him alive all these years. He should have died ten times over by now. Although anger had saved him many times over, eventually, it would lead to his demise. Daniel had worked so hard to keep his anger under control. While he stared at the wisps of smoke, he wondered why it was becoming increasingly difficult for him to discover what had happened here and why. Why did the villagers push him out of the burning rubble? Why did the abbot want him arrested? Why were the mercenaries in the tavern? Why did Brian's wife interrupt just when Brian was going to tell Daniel what he knew?

Some force prevented Daniel from gathering the information he needed to discover what had happened to his love. Every time he got close to a truth, something chased him off or took the information away from him. The more Daniel thought of it, the angrier he got. He would have to become more aggressive in finding the truth.

The first thing that needed to be done was to free Brian from his wife. Daniel turned and walked swiftly back to Brian's cottage. The sun was above the horizon. Daniel knocked. After a while, the door creaked open, and Ann stood in the doorway.

"What do you want? Shouldn't you be home sleeping it off the way my man is doing right now?"

"Misses, I don't have much time. I need your husband awake."

"So do I, but he is a good-for-nothing drunk who—"

"I don't care what he is to you. I need him. He has valuable information that I require."

"Wait a minute. I knew there was something familiar about you. I didn't notice it in the darkness, but now in the light—yes, you *are* him."

Daniel pushed his way in. "Please, keep your voice down."

"Get out! Get out, right this instant! How dare you!

You cannot just go barging into people's homes! If you do not leave this instant you will leave me no other choice—"

She didn't have a chance to finish her sentence as Daniel clamped his hand over her mouth and pushed her into the kitchen area, "I do not have time for this. You know who I am?" She nodded.

"Then you know I would never harm peaceful people like yourself." She nodded again.

"Mommy, Mommy ... "The little girl's voice trailed off. "Wow, it's him. It's the Opal Knight!"

A knock at the door drew Daniel's attention. "Are you expecting company?" Ann shook her head no.

Daniel heard whispers, indicating that the visitor at the door was not alone. A low whisper from the back room caused Daniel to draw his dagger and turn.

"Wait. Wait. It's me. Come on. Follow me."

It was Brian. As Daniel turned toward him, Brian raised his empty hands. Brian waved his right hand for Daniel to follow. Daniel had no choice. Other than Macha and Balor, Brian was the closest person he had as an ally right now. Of course, hearing the door pushed open by those visitors helped make his decision clearer. He quickly ran through the kitchen into the back room of the cottage. The back door was open, and he moved toward it when his ankle was grabbed by a hand from below. It was Brian. He was in a hideaway below the floor of the cottage. Without any thought, Daniel hopped into the hole, and Brian covered it back up with the false floor. Two pairs of feet ran over them and out the opened back door.

Slightly hunched over, Brian made his way at an angle that appeared perpendicular to the layout of the cottage.

Daniel followed in a more uncomfortable bent position. He had to bend almost at the waist to avoid hitting his head on the ceiling of the tunnel. Torches spaced equidistant apart in the walls lit the way. Daniel had traveled many places and heard that in some villages, the people had developed a unique method of surviving raids. They made these types of tunnels for escape or evasion, but he did not know that Lough Inch was ever one of those towns until now.

Daniel followed Brian for a good while, it seemed. Brian turned and gave him that all-too-familiar finger to lips sign to keep quiet. Daniel crouched as Brian ever so carefully lifted the false floor of their exit slightly. Daniel could see Brian peering around for any activity. A deep growl from above caused Brian to fall back onto Daniel.

Daniel pushed Brian off of him. "What is it?"

"A terrible beast. We must be in the forest where those terrible creatures dwell. I knew I should have made that first right—or left. Dammit! If I only knew my right from my left." Brian continued his mumbling.

Daniel just shook his head in disbelief. Daniel took out his dagger and placed it in his left hand to pry open the false floor. He drew his short sword in anticipation of fighting his way out of the hole. As Daniel cautiously pried open the cover with his dagger, he noticed two huge, furry feet attached to death-black, thick, troll-like legs. The legs connected to the thick, brown neck of a huge beast. Was this a troll? Or some other beast from hell?

CHAPTER 7

Daniel not only felt the warmth of the beast's breath, but the stench of its breath overwhelmed him. However, he gathered all of his courage and pushed his way through the opening. Brian reached for Daniel's left foot not so much to save his life but so as not to remain behind in the tunnel with a troll lurking so close. The troll had Brian's scent. It would only be a matter of time before it came for him, once it killed and ate Daniel. Brian kept still and listened. He tried to determine whether Daniel was still alive. He heard no clash of metal cleaving muscle and sinew into bone, nor did he hear any bone shattering from the massive fists of the troll. The silence could only mean one thing—Daniel was dead. Brian panicked. He would be next. The troll would smash his huge, club-like hands through the floorboards and snatch Brian up by his neck. He had to escape. He had to figure out where to go. He could go back to his cottage, but their pursuers might still be prowling.

Capture was a better alternative than what waited for him with the troll. Brian bent down and turned to head back when the false floor flew open and two large, strong hands gripped him by his shoulders, squeezed, and pulled him up through the floor. As Brian opened his mouth to let out a cry for help, a hand wrapped around his mouth, thus stifling a scream for assistance.

Brian fought as best he could. He flailed his arms and legs wildly in an attempt to free himself from the most horrid of deaths. The image of a troll gnawing on him as if he were a chicken nauseated him. A thump of a huge foot and a growl from beneath his flailing foot caused Brian to resign himself to his fate. However, he would not die face down in a puddle of his own vomit after another night of drunken debauchery. No, Brian would prove his wife wrong. He would die slowly as the troll ripped him apart and ate him piece by piece, limb by limb.

I'd rather lose another argument, Brian thought.

Brian slowly opened one eye and then the other. The barn was dark and damp. He could barely make out the shape of the walls. At least the monster had the courtesy to face Brian away so he could not witness himself being ripped apart and eaten. The beast slowly turned Brian around and released the iron grip on his shoulders. Brian dropped to the floor and realized that Daniel had grabbed him, not a monster. The knight's horse and dog were standing on either side of him, and Brian swore to himself that the dog smiled in amusement.

Brian still trembled when Daniel spoke. "My friend, it's okay. All friends here, no trolls or monsters. You have a wild imagination, Brian."

"Yeah, well, you never came face to face with a troll before. Have you, oh brave knight?"

"Calm yourself, my friend. I've witnessed things in my life that you wish were only nightmares. Now quiet, a small contingent of the guard just headed in the direction of your cottage. I wish I knew why everyone was after me."

"What do you mean everyone? Who else is after you?"

"Nothing, I meant nothing by it. Just a weary traveler's paranoia that's all."

"Daniel, please do not insult my intelligence. Well, don't insult my common sense at least. I know you are not a weary traveler. The strength in your hands, the way you carry yourself—yes, you instinctively changed your posture when the guards knocked at my door. And there was the unusual interest in the witch's cottage."

"She is … was not a witch!"

"Aha! I knew it! You are the Opa—" Brian could not finish the sentence as Daniel's thumb and forefinger squeezed an area just to the right of the throat and above the clavicle.

"Be quiet, or I will fix it so that you are unable to speak, or write, or make gestures. Am I clear?" Daniel whispered through clenched teeth into Brian's face.

Daniel continued. "Now, I'm going to remove my hand. You are not to utter one sound. Just nod your head if you understand."

Brian nodded, and Daniel removed his hand.

"I need to know right now—no hesitation, no thought—are you with me?"

Brian nodded.

"Good. Now we have to get out of town. I can't keep wasting time evading capture when it can be spent thinking through what has happened. You can talk now, but whisper."

"Where will you—we go?"

"Don't worry about that. Once we can get away from here, I will know where to go."

"The guards won't stop looking until they find us. Nightfall is hours away, and we cannot stay hidden that long. The longer it takes to find us, the more reinforcements will be called in to help."

"You're right. We have several choices to make here."

"Um, several?"

"Several. First, we can give ourselves up. We both would

face prosecution and possibly torture for whatever crime I am being hunted for."

"Wait, what do you mean *we*?"

"You aided in my escape, so you most assuredly would be tried as an accessory."

Tears began to well up in Brian's eyes, and his bottom lip quivered at the thought of torture.

"Second," Daniel continued, "we can evade capture by remaining hidden and attempt escape once night falls. That, too, has the strong possibility of the same outcome as our first option."

The tears streamed down Brian's cheeks.

"Third, we can fight our way out of town. I'm sure we would fight bravely and legendary tales would be told of our heroic attempt at escape."

"Attempt at escape?" Brian's shoulders shook uncontrollably.

"The ideal choice is to flee, evade detection, avoid capture, and escape."

"I like that one." Brian wiped his tears with his stained sleeves.

Balor growled. Daniel and Brian turned toward the barn door as it slowly creaked open. It seemed the choice would be made sooner than Daniel expected.

Brian shook uncontrollably. Daniel drew his short sword for the close-quarters fight he felt was upon them. At the same time, he knelt and gave Balor the signal to stay quiet. Silence was their ally. Whoever entered the barn did not know they were there. It was just a search. If they knew the barn housed the fugitives, a much larger contingent would have swarmed them by now.

Balor moved into position several feet away from the door. Macha backed into an opposite corner of where Daniel stood. Daniel crouched, ready to spring on whoever entered. Brian stood frozen in fear. They all stared at the door in anticipation of what they would do once it opened. Balor, Macha, and Daniel all knew their role once the door opened.

Balor would lay down on the floor while Macha would rear up, thus confusing the intruder. Daniel would then have that instant to assess the true threat and take appropriate action. Brian was the determining factor of the outcome. Daniel, Macha, and Balor had shared so many experiences together for so long that all three knew exactly the capabilities of each. All Daniel knew about Brian was that he was a heavy drinker who was soft. But Daniel also suspected that Brian had some skill. He seemed resourceful.

The heavy, wooden barn door opened wider. It creaked and shuddered as a large gauntlet pushed it open. The guard opened the door with great caution. Daniel knew this guard was well trained, but he was not one of the town guards. As the guard exposed more of his arm, Daniel observed that he one of the elite guards of the abbey. Daniel concluded that the conspiracy ran deep. He began to understand as pieces of this puzzle fell into place.

The door pushed a few more inches open, and the point of a poleax halberd entered first followed by the large shaft. The guard held the weapon with both hands, ready to keep whatever he encountered at bay until aid arrived. Daniel peered through the crack the door made between the wooden door itself and the doorjamb and confirmed that the guard was alone. The rest of the guard force was in the middle of a standard house-to-house search. It seemed odd that this guard was alone.

A squad of guards consisting of six to ten men conducted house-to-house searches. Half of the contingent would go inside in pairs to conduct a thorough search, while the rest remained outside forming a perimeter to prevent escape or to support the guards inside should they meet resistance.

Daniel could think of only two possible reasons why this guard was alone: he had acted under some secret orders from the abbot or time was a factor. It's possible that both reasons could explain why this guard was alone. The point of the halberd continued its probe into the dimly lit barn. The guard's eyes followed the rays of the sun as they slowly walked across the dirty straw strewn on the barn floor. The sunlight rested upon the body of the mastiff. Balor remained perfectly still. Macha reared up, snorted, and landed with a loud thud. The guard shifted his gaze away from mastiff toward the sound to his right, giving Daniel the opening he needed.

Daniel grabbed the shaft of the halberd between the end of the pike and the head of the ax. He pulled the guard off balance and into the barn. Brian came to his wits and quickly moved to close the barn door so the disturbance would go unseen by the other guards. Balor leaped up and out of the way while his master did his work.

Daniel tossed the halberd away and landed on the guard's back. His knees pressed onto the upper arms of the guard and immobilized him. Even without his mouth gagged, the guard could not cry out for help. He struggled to breathe as the full weight of the knight rested on his back. Daniel removed the guard's helm. Balor crouched low in front of the guard's face, snarling. Daniel pulled the guard by the hair and lifted his head so he could see the mastiff's snarl.

Daniel quickly looked to ensure that Macha was okay and then continued his scan around the barn to locate Brian. Daniel found him sitting on the floor with his back against the door.

"Brian, come here. I have a plan."

"But … but I'm watching the door."

"Dammit, get over here, you sniveling coward."

Brian couldn't bring himself to his feet, so he crawled on all fours to Daniel.

"Remove his uniform."

"What? I'm not doing that."

The guard wriggled to resist. Balor growled, and the wriggling ceased.

"Brian, he is the same size, more or less, as you."

"Okay, so what? Plenty of people are my size."

"You will put the uniform on and act as if you have captured me. When we clear the guard force, we make our escape out of town."

"Ah, I get it now."

As Brian grabbed the guard's right boot, he kicked out, sending Brian flailing. He almost dislodged Daniel, but Daniel sent a closed fist to the base of the guard's neck, effectively eliminating any more resistance.

Daniel and Brian worked quickly to remove the guard's uniform and get it on Brian. It was a little snug because Brian refused to remove any of his own clothing other than his tunic. While Brian dressed, Daniel moved the guard into a stall near the back of the barn out of sight. He bound his hands to his ankles and placed a soiled rag he found into the guard's mouth. Once Brian finished dressing, Daniel reviewed the plan with him.

Brian would assume the role of the guard who managed to capture the Opal Knight. Daniel would lay across Macha's saddle seemingly unconscious, with his hands bound. Brian would lead Macha and his "captive" through the town toward the abbey. Daniel made it clear to Brian that he must go right upon exiting the barn. Daniel pointed, recalling Brian's confession of not knowing his right from his left.

"What difference does it make?"

"All the difference for our escape. Either direction will take the same amount time and cover the same distance toward the abbey. However, if you go left, we will be further away from the town entrance and the direction of our escape route."

"What about the dog?"

"Balor will remain behind."

"Don't you think we should have him with us in case we get into any trouble?"

"All the more reason for him to stay behind."

"That did not answer my question." Brian made the final adjustments to his uniform and stood for inspection.

Daniel adjusted the helm just enough to conceal Brian's eyes and the nose guard to help shadow his face.

"Now, take the halberd and show me how you walk."

"How I walk? You've seen how I walk."

"Yes, I have. Now I need to see how you walk like a man, not a groveling, beat-down, drunken husband of an abusive wife."

Brian opened his mouth to challenge Daniel's description

but realized that all he heard was the truth. Brian snatched up the halberd, placed it in his right hand, and stood as soldier-like as possible.

"Hmm, not quite. Stand straighter. Shoulders back. Head up. A soldier is always looking around unless marching. Do not look toward the ground."

"Yes, but in this town, if you look someone in their eyes, you are asking for a fight."

"True, but you are a guard now. Act like one. A guard or soldier is always looking for a fight."

Daniel took his time with Brian. Even though time was not on their side, if Brian did not act the part, the plan would fail. After several minutes of training in basic soldier and guard skills, Daniel felt it was time to execute his plan.

They got Macha ready. Before Daniel mounted her, he knelt down to face Balor. He whispered and made subtle hand gestures that only he and Balor understood. He gave Balor a hug around his neck and put his nose to Balor's nose so that both master and dog could look into each other's eyes. Daniel stood and gave Balor one final pat on the side of neck. Balor moved toward the entrance of the barn where he could see out. From this vantage point, Balor would observe his master as long as possible.

Daniel mounted Macha and laid across her back facing the ground. Brian handed Daniel some rope so he could wrap his wrists to appear bound. Brian inhaled deeply, gathered what little courage he could find, opened the barn door, led Macha out by her reins, and headed toward the right and freedom.

Brian focused on his role. He made sure he pushed his shoulders back, held the halberd in his right hand, kept his arm at a near-perfect right angle, and walked a steady pace with purpose. Although Daniel faced the ground and was unable to lift his head to see where they were, he concentrated and relied on his other senses to provide him the information he needed. By the smell, he could tell they neared the market and were close to the center of town. Hearing also gave him vital information. The clanging of trinkets validated that the marketplace was nearby. His hearing also picked up the rhythmic footsteps of the town guard. The sound grew louder and louder until all of a sudden they stopped, as did Macha.

"Hold! What do you have here?" a voice of authority asked.

Brian delayed and tried to remember what Daniel had told him to say if they should be stopped and questioned.

Daniel heard one set of steps move closer. "What do you have *there*?" the same voice asked, annoyed that he had to repeat himself.

Brian struggled, but it finally came to him. "I got him. I captured the Opal Knight."

The guard force whispered among themselves and suddenly ceased as the sergeant of the guard gave them a quick glance to get back in formation.

"What do you mean *captured*? Those were not the orders I received."

Brian worried. He stalled while he gathered his composure along with his thoughts. "Is that so? What orders did you receive? Because mine were quite clear."

Meanwhile, Daniel remained perfectly still hoping Brian could get through this.

"Never mind my orders. I'm the sergeant of the guard. You will answer my question."

The sergeant gave the hand signal for the formation to break ranks and take up positions on either side of the horse and captor. They were well trained and knew that a horse of this size could easily trample anyone in front of it and cause serious damage to anyone standing behind with its rear hooves.

Brian responded in his most authoritarian voice, "You might be the sergeant of the guard, but I am a soldier of the Church. My orders come from God through the abbot."

"The abbot?" the sergeant of the guard asked, doubting his decision to delay any soldier under orders from the abbot.

"Yes, the abbot. Now, unless you wish the ire of the abbot to be brought down upon you, I suggest you let me complete my task so I can go home."

The sergeant of the guard stepped aside and gave the signal for his guards to fall back into formation. Brian thanked him and led Macha past the guard force. As Brian and Daniel breathed a sigh of relief, the sergeant of the guard deployed his force in a similar manner, but this time their weapons were drawn and at the ready.

The sergeant stood there and smiled with his hands on his hips. "Imposter, drop the reins and step away from the horse."

"Imposter? How dare you!" Brian tried his best to put on the guise of an insulted soldier.

"Yes, imposter. You almost got away with it. It wasn't until you told me you wanted to go home that I realized you were an imposter. I must commend you on your fine acting, imposter, but soldiers of the Church live in the abbey."

"Acting? What are you talking about? Step aside. I must get to the abbey."

"Release the reins and step away from the horse!" the sergeant commanded.

"I will not! I am on a mission from the abbot." Brian's voice cracked under the stress of being caught. He delayed as best he could and gave Daniel time to come his rescue.

CHAPTER 8

Daniel prayed that the sergeant of the guard had not become aware of the error in Brian's lie, but he had. They would have to fight their way out of this or their freedom and, perhaps, even their lives would be lost. He subtly moved his hands to his mouth and gently blew three quick, short breaths through his fingertips.

Two guards moved toward Brian and seized him by the arms. Another attempted to grab Macha's reins, but she moved away from the guard. Macha's sudden movement caused the entire guard force to take steps away from the large animal. Brian wriggled out of the guard's grip and moved toward Macha. Daniel slid off the horse in a heap, maintaining the guise of the prisoner. All the guards had their short swords drawn, and Brian stood next Macha. Daniel moaned softly and drew the attention of the sergeant.

The townspeople stirred, and some moved toward the disturbance. Recent events concerning jurisdictional boundaries between the town guard and the abbey had strained relations between the two forces. Many townspeople lived out a meager existence and were always up for a fight between the two. The sergeant of the guard realized that he would soon be challenged with crowd control as well as dealing with an extremely dangerous criminal.

"Imposter, calm your horse. We don't want to make this messy for you or your animal, but we will if we must. Let's just both return to the guardhouse and sort this out. I'm sure we can come to some—"

He did not finish his negotiation. The crowd disbursed suddenly as a huge form bowled over one of the guards and bounded right onto the sergeant, pushing him to the ground. Daniel stood up and removed his own short sword from the sheath on Macha's saddle. The point barely touched the skin under the chin of the sergeant.

"No one move! Drop your weapons!"

The guard force maintained their ready posture.

"Sergeant, I have no argument with you. I understand you and your men are duty bound to follow orders, but I am desperate."

"Knight, you know I cannot give the order to have my men drop their weapons. Do you know what would happen to me if I showed an act of cowardice while under orders? I will be stripped of my rank, flogged in public, and my family subjected to humiliation and indentured."

"Hmm, seems that we are at a stalemate. You are being used, but I do not want you or your family to suffer for what is certainly a plot to destroy me. However, I must leave this town and find my love. I know someone has her."

"The witch? She's dead."

"She is not a witch! Nor is she dead," Daniel stammered, controlling his temper.

Daniel grabbed the sergeant by his tunic and lifted him to his feet. The guards stepped back with their weapons still drawn, knowing what Daniel was capable of doing. They had all heard the tales, and although some of them were quite farfetched, they knew that all tales and legends are based on fact. Some of the guards had witnessed the Opal Knight in a drunken rage and knew he was ten times more deadly sober.

Daniel pulled the sergeant closer to him. The edge of the blade pressed against the sergeant's throat now. The sergeant's hands raised in surrender. He felt the desperation in the knight's grip and, although Daniel told him he did not want to hurt him, the sergeant knew he would if he felt threatened. As Daniel backed closer to Macha, Balor assumed a defensive position on the opposite side of the horse to prevent any attempt of attack from the rear.

Daniel motioned for Brian to get on the horse. As Brian put his foot in the stirrup and mounted, his helm fell to the ground. The sound caused the sergeant to turn his head toward Brian.

"Wait. You look familiar …"

"Yes, we have established that already. I am the Opal Knight," Daniel responded.

"No … "The last word was uttered as the halberd that Brian held found its way between two ribs and pierced the sergeant's lung.

The sergeant gurgled. Dark, red blood—so dark that it appeared black—bubbled in his mouth. He collapsed. His full weight fell on the blade that Daniel still held against his throat, adding a partial decapitation to the collapsed lung. Daniel saw his opportunity to escape as the guards stood in shock and watched the life drain from their sergeant's body. Daniel mounted Macha behind Brian, took hold of the reins, and gave Macha the subtle command to flee as Balor kept pace.

They made their escape from the village. The group fled east at full speed for at least a half hour toward the great forest. As they cleared the crest of the hill leading east away from Lough Inch, Daniel steered Macha north into the dense forest. He felt that their pursuers would believe they fled east toward the coast away from the reach of the abbot. They would not consider the dense forest as an avenue of escape since it would slow the party down. Once Daniel felt that they had pushed deep enough into the forest, and out of immediate danger, he slowed Macha to a steady gait to give her time to recuperate. As the sun made its trek across the sky and the forest grew thicker, both Daniel and Brian dismounted and walked on either side of Macha. Balor scouted ahead and found a small clearing that appeared to be a good place to remove the saddle from the great Frisian and for both to rest. Daniel now had time to recount the events that had led up to their present predicament.

Several questions disturbed Daniel: Why did the sergeant seem to recognize him a second time? *Perhaps the sergeant was just stalling for time.* How did Brian manage to kill the sergeant with no training in that particular weapon? *Brian did stumble; the uniform did not fit him exactly. Stroke of luck, good or bad, Brian's accidentally killing the sergeant gave them the perfect distraction to escape.* Daniel signaled that it was time to ready for departure.

Daniel led the party deeper and farther north until night approached. Macha and Balor sensed his anxiety. Daniel searched for a place they could safely rest for the night. The party relied on Daniel's familiarity with this forest. As the sun completed its journey, Daniel gave the order to halt and dismount. He led them to a hidden cave for shelter.

Balor disappeared into the nearby trees to scout. Macha stood by while Daniel relieved her of the saddle. Brian gathered some dead branches to start a fire. When he thought he had gathered enough, he returned to the cave entrance, dropped the kindling, and sat down.

"That will not be enough," Daniel said.

"That's more than enough. It will get us through the night and then some."

Daniel was rubbing down Macha and turned. "Gather more wood, please."

"Are you serious? I'm exhausted."

Daniel stopped brushing Macha and looked at him. Brian stacked the wood he had gathered into a loose pile. He felt very uncomfortable, turned, and looked up into the eyes of the knight. The same eyes that moments ago were anxious, yet relieved, now appeared angry and focused upon him. Without a word, Brian bounced to his feet and headed back to the forest to gather additional wood. He returned to the cave entrance with more wood until Daniel indicated that he had accumulated enough.

"Knight, where is your dog? I have not seen him for some time."

"He is nearby. Now get inside the cave."

The cave was deep enough and high enough for Macha to stand inside comfortably, but Daniel ensured that she could roam free outside if she chose. Most likely she would stay near the cave entrance changing positions with Balor providing inner security. This was the method most commonly used when the group was being pursued. It gave Daniel ample time to saddle Macha while Balor kept any intruders or attackers occupied. They were thirsty and hungry but could only manage to fill their skins with water from a nearby stream, which Daniel tasked Brian to handle. The darker it got, the more wood Daniel put on the fire, and he never ventured from the halo of light the fire produced. They quenched their thirst, but the intensity of their hunger pangs sharpened. Balor found some mice to sate his huge appetite, and Macha grazed her fill. Daniel and Brian, however, remained hungry. As hungry as Daniel was, he would not venture away from the safety of the fire, and Brian was not a hunter.

Brian complained to himself how hungry he was but shortly hunkered down in the back of the cave. Macha grazed with a watchful eye always on the knight as he slowly paced around the fire until, at last, he felt secure enough to sit facing the cave entrance. The knight soon wrapped himself in his cloak, and he drifted off to sleep. Balor sensed his master's tension. The great mastiff tightened his perimeter so he could better monitor his master as well as perform his security duty.

Daniel drifted into a deep sleep, but while his body rested, his mind still worked. He soon returned to the same dream that tormented him. It started at the same point but moved more quickly to the point he woke the last time.

Daniel walked through the village toward the church. Walking the path was still a struggle, but he was being pulled and had to get to the church. The frustration and anger came back in a rush, but he looked for his peace and found her. Everything was the same except the stained-glass windows. Something was different. The stained-glass figures moved as before. The hag still stirred the boiling cauldron. Saint Patrick still chased the snakes. However, the image of the knight on horseback with his dog running alongside had changed. The dog was in the air as if to pounce in ambush on the unsuspecting knight.

Daniel felt a chill run down his spine as if a dog was behind him, and he turned, sword drawn as if to ward off an unprovoked ambush. As he turned, he looked to see the third stained-glass window of Cassandra and him explode. The explosion sent shards of glass flying throughout the church as before. The crying eye found its way to Daniel's feet. As he looked in disbelief at the frame, one piece still dangled, but several pieces were pulled back into the framework. A finger, cross, and the knight's opal now joined the once lone, dangling piece. The four pieces were not where they belonged in the lattice; instead, they turned this way and that, seemingly forcing themselves into place next to one another. It didn't make sense. Daniel moved his lips and tried to tell the pieces where they belonged in the window, but he had no voice. The entire scene ignored Daniel. He became frustrated again, more from being ignored than not understanding what was happening.

Daniel slept restlessly the remainder of the night and awoke at a nuzzle of Macha. He stretched, sat up, and looked around. He felt the chill of the morning air. The fire had died out in the night, and his clothing was a little damp from the early morning dew. Daniel noticed that Brian was not in the cave or within the inner perimeter that Daniel had mentally diagrammed. He sprung up and drew his sword. Macha dug up clods of earth with her hooves as she often did when nervous.

All kinds of thoughts ran through Daniel's mind. *Where is Brian? Was he taken in the middle of the night? Did he run away?*

"Sir Knight! Sir Knight!"

Daniel's attention was drawn to the tree line where Brian stood frantically waving his arms to draw Daniel's attention. He ran toward Brian, drawing his free hand across his throat to tell Brian to be quiet. Daniel still was unsure whether they were safe or not. He assumed the worst—that the town guard or the legion from the abbey had found them. Where was Balor? Clearly, he should have heard the commotion by now. As Daniel scanned the forest a familiar shadow appeared. Apparently, as the sun broke the horizon, Balor extended his defensive perimeter.

As Daniel neared Brian's location, Brian turned and ran up and over the rise. Daniel closed the gap and within seconds was on Brian's heels. Brian turned, smiled, and pointed toward the bottom of the hill.

At the bottom of the hill grew dozens of wild berry bushes. Daniel and Brian ate their fill and picked enough to fill their satchels. The party continued on its way to a location known only to the knight, but Brian relentlessly asked questions. He wondered why, if they were to find Cassandra, they trekked farther and farther away from the source of her kidnapping and murder. Who were they going to see? Where was this person's location? The more questions Brian asked, the more Daniel's suspicion grew about Brian's true purpose.

They traveled for three more days, and each night they sought shelter in pretty much the same fashion as the first. As each night passed, Brian wandered farther away from camp on "solo hunting expeditions" for longer periods of time, often returning well after the moon had risen. Each day, Daniel led them on trails that wound, sometimes going in one direction and then, for no particular reason, Daniel would lead the party in a totally different direction.

On the fourth day, prior to Brian's usual early wake-up,

he received a blow to his head. When he woke, he realized he was bound and was terrified. He knew he had been attacked, but by whom? Where was the knight? Why hadn't the mastiff given warning, or the warhorse for that matter?

As he struggled with his binds, he realized he could not see, hear, or smell. Had the fiends who attacked them gouged out his eyes? Cut off his ears? As his head throbbed, he deduced what had happened. During the night, a vicious band of highwaymen that had been tracking them had finally seized the opportunity. The robbers and murderers dispatched the dog so it would not sound the alarm. He was knocked unconscious as the knight attempted to ward off the attack, probably being killed or severely maimed during the melee. The thieves took the horse, and now Brian was going to be taken to some remote location to be sold as a slave, probably to the Moors. Brian shuddered at the thought. He recalled the horrifying stories told by the Crusaders of what happened to slaves in the homes of the Moors.

Meanwhile, Daniel, Balor, and Macha just watched Brian as he struggled. Daniel recalled what had prompted him to seize Brian. There had been something different about Brian since that night they had escaped and avoided the tower guard. Why would a seemingly harmless merchant and drunk have access to a labyrinth of secret tunnels under his cottage that extended beyond the limits of the village? Why would Brian agree to go with him on such a perilous journey? How could the merchant have known how to make a death blow with such an unlikely weapon? How was someone not adept in forestry or hunting able to serve fresh game for dinner each night? Why did he disappear each night for increasing lengths of time? Why was Brian asking such detailed questions?

Finally, the previous night, Daniel had decided that there were way too many coincidences. Since the knight did not believe in coincidences, or in a collection of random acts coinciding to produce a particular outcome, Daniel's paranoia went into overdrive. Paranoia was deeply ingrained in Daniel's soul and often proved to be his personal life saver. Daniel left Brian bound, gagged, and blindfolded, with his ears and nose plugged under Balor's watchful eye. Daniel continued to his destination on Macha.

Daniel recalled the first visit he had made to this place as an adolescent. It was in the spring of perhaps his eleventh year. He had continued his visits to Cassandra, and he grew in height and strength toward manhood; she had grown into a young woman. Daniel's visits became longer but never lasted past sundown. Cassandra's mother never allowed Daniel's visits to last any longer, and that was fine with Daniel. It was odd how, as Cassandra's mother grew more tolerant of Daniel, Cassandra retreated into herself. After a while Daniel didn't seem to mind, as long as he could be with his love.

Then it happened.

The local constabulary made its annual "recruitment" of young men of fighting age. The usual term was two years away from home, and the boys/men would then have a choice to stay in the local militia, work on a merchant vessel, or serve God at an abbey for two additional years. Daniel did not particularly care for any choices, but he did not have a say. Daniel was destined for greatness, and he knew it. He decided that two years away from the path laid out before him would not do, so he fled. He did not take into consideration his friends or the girl he loved. Even though he did not know he loved her, he knew that each time he thought about her or saw her, time stood still. The choice was difficult, but he knew that if he did not make his escape immediately, he would be seized and taken to the training camps far away from Lough Inch.

He knew he should have explained his plan to his friends, family, and love, but the less they knew, the better his chances were. Daniel fled deep into the forest away from his home, village, and any neighboring towns. His trek led him across several streams, through thick forests, across wide open fields, and over several hills. He traveled for two days. He slept only when he could not walk anymore. His sleeps were restless, cold, and filled with nightmares. The nightmares differed. Some were of him being chased by the banshee, while others had him under the influence of a witch. But all ended the same way: him seized by the shoulders and pulled to his feet. It was always during this part of the dream that Daniel would jump awake. He would be disoriented, but once he rubbed the sleep from his eyes, he would recall his immediate concern—flee!

At midmorning on the third day, as Daniel approached the crest of yet another hill—how many hills did Ireland have?—he heard a strange language in a stranger-sounding voice. The voice was that of a man chanting or singing. Daniel quickly dropped behind the trunk of one of the hundreds of oak trees that dominated this part of the country. The voice stopped. Daniel dared not move for fear of discovery. The chanting started again, and Daniel crept closer to the crest of the hill. He certainly did not recognize this part of the country, and as Daniel attempted to gain his bearings, he feared he was lost.

CHAPTER 9

Young Daniel was confused. He thought he knew his way in and around all the forests within three days travel of the village. He had left Lough Inch only two days before so he should not be lost, yet here he was on an unfamiliar knoll, surrounded by unfamiliar trees, and watching an unfamiliar man. The stranger was much shorter than most men in Lough Inch—as a matter of fact, than most men in Ireland. A gray or dirty white robe covered his frail frame. It was difficult to distinguish which. A strong rope cinched tight at the waist kept the robe tight to his body. A completely bald head protruded through the top of the robe. A long, gray beard speckled with black flecks covered most of his wrinkled face, but his upper lip was bare. Young Daniel could not tell the color of the old man's eyes. Gnarled hands that extended from the sleeves of the robe held a long, wooden staff. It appeared sturdy enough to support the old man while he walked or stood. Strangely it also looked as though the stranger could easily convert the staff into a weapon as necessary. Simple sandals protected his feet.

The camp was simple. A pot that contained his food for the day hung over the fire. Kindling was piled near a lean-to that was set up in the center of a glade protected by mighty oaks and large, oblong stones encircling it. It gave the appearance that a giant's hand held the camp in his palm. His large, stone fingers jutted from the earth.

The man chanted in much softer tones, barely audible to Daniel's sharp ears. Daniel still kept out of sight and made sure that he did not make any sounds. He had to hear what this old man was chanting. He leaned closer so he could hear a little better, but the words were still unintelligible.

He shifted his weight ever so slightly, but the rocks gave way and he tumbled down the hill. He felt as if he rolled forever, picking up scrapes and bruises along the way The steep grade leveled off, and Daniel slowly rolled to a stop just at the outside edge of the stone circle. Even up close, Daniel's assessment had been accurate. They looked like giant fingers.

Daniel laid perfectly still and hoped beyond hope that the old man did not hear or see him. Daniel still did not understand any of the words the man chanted even though he could now hear clearly. He decided he would try to lift himself up to a crouch and steal away back to the trees and out of sight. One of the giant fingers blocked his line of sight, but it sounded as if the old man was on the other side of the circle across the glade. Daniel planned to crouch, peek around the finger, and confirm that the old man was facing away from him, at which point he would run low toward the edge of the trees. After a few more seconds, Daniel would execute his plan.

One, two, three … but Daniel did not move. It wasn't that he didn't want to move. He couldn't. Daniel did a quick self-check. He felt the aches and pains from the bumps and bruises he had acquired from his tumble, so he was not paralyzed. He just could not move. He could move his eyes, wiggle his nostrils, and open his mouth. He just could not command his muscles to move according to his plan. Something was not right. Daniel continued to try and will his body to move, but he failed.

The chanting ceased, and Daniel heard footsteps. Daniel thought, *How stupid am I? I'm going to die here and no one will know about it. I could have easily dealt with two years in military training. Who knows? Maybe I would—*

The old man stood over young Daniel and interrupted his thoughts. He spoke a language Daniel could not understand. It sounded much like Gaelic but had a harsher, sharper tone and accent. The words came quicker and seemed to run together. Daniel was certain this old man was not happy to see him. The old man stood upright, muttered something to himself, and looked back at Daniel. In a language and dialect common to Daniel's village, the old man asked several questions.

"Why are you here? How did you find me? Are you a spy? Where are the others?"

Daniel was able to respond, "Please, sir, I meant no harm. I am lost. Please help me. I can't seem to move. I may have broken something. I can't move any muscles."

"Untrue. Your tongue is a muscle. I knew you were coming, Toad."

With that simple decision to flee recruitment from the constabulary, Daniel's path to become the Opal Knight began.

Daniel pushed his memories back and brought himself to the here and now. He neared the crest of the hill and looked for the sign he was taught all those years ago, the sign showing him he was in the right location. There it was. Undetectable, if one did not know what he looked for, it seemed like an ordinary, gnarled, tree branch windswept into a strange, curved position. He approached the branch and caressed the trunk of the ancient oak. This tree told him so many things. Most importantly, the old man waited for him on the other side. The other side revealed itself to Daniel.

Daniel passed through the curtain of branches and leaves as they made way for him. As he stepped through, he arrived only steps away from the very spot where he had met the old man all those years ago. The old man stepped from the circle of stone fingers and reached for Daniel's hand.

"Toad, it is good to see you. I've felt your many successes all these years. You have become a good man. Hmm, but you are troubled. Someone you love dearly has been taken from you."

Daniel could never hide his true feelings from his mentor and did not even try to this time.

Daniel knelt on his right knee. "Yes, Athair. It is Cassandra. She has been taken. At first I thought she was killed, but now I think the Church took her. In the past, she has been accused of practicing witchcraft, but no evidence has ever been brought against her. I fear she will be tried and put to death."

"Not true."

"What do you mean, *not true?*"

"Yes."

Daniel started but recalled that it was fruitless to continue to question the old man. It had always been his way. This is how Daniel learned and grew. He had to discover the answer himself. The rewards were always greater when Daniel discovered the truth he sought himself. Athair would only guide him. Daniel formulated a question to propose to the old man, his Athair, in order to find out if he was heading in the right direction. Daniel stood up.

"Athair, I must know where to start to look for

Cassandra. So my question to you is this: if I continue my present course, how many days' walk will it take for me to find her?"

"Even a toad would not survive. Farewell, Mac."

Daniel became upset and angry—not at the old man, but at himself. In his desperation to save his Cassandra, Daniel realized that he had asked his question in haste and had not thought it out. It had taken Daniel many years to learn the old man's methods of answering questions, but his mind was so clouded that he failed to remember the method and, therefore, failed to get an answer. He decided to try one more time.

"Athair, please, I am desperate and distraught. I have nowhere else to turn. Every time I turn around, a new enemy emerges. Please give me some direction."

"Mac, you know that is not the way, and besides, I gave you the answer you need."

Daniel was still lost but did not get angry or show his disappointment. He just knelt down before the old man, received his blessing, rose, and went back the way he had come. Every lesson the old man had taught Daniel could never be repaid except to give him the unconditional love only a son could give. Daniel turned and waved. The old man returned a smile and a nod.

Daniel proceeded through the hidden entrance back to where he had left Macha, Balor, and their prisoner. The three had hardly moved since Daniel left to visit with the old man. Balor was on guard, and Macha stood on Brian's tunic, pinning him to the ground in a sitting position. Dusk settled in, and Daniel built the usual fire. They all braced themselves for the arrival of darkness.

Daniel became more distraught as he thought about Athair's response to his question. He could not decipher the old man's message: *"Even a toad would not survive."* Thoughts of his love being tortured to death in a variety of methods crept into Daniel's mind.

He stared up into the night sky as he laid close to the fire. As he watched the few clouds drift by, the light from millions of stars found him. Soon, Daniel drifted off to sleep, and he dreamt. This time his dream had nothing to do with the church or the shattered stained-glass windows or the images. This dream was about his reunion with the old man. The dream showed the meeting with the old man from all different angles—first from the old man's perspective, then Daniel's, then that of an insect crawling along the ground, then that of a bird that just landed onto one of the large stones, and finally, from the perspective of the large tree that overlooked the entire scene. Even the conversations were strange. They were loud and then whispered, they seemed to proceed backward, and then they came from above. Macha moved closer to her master and nuzzled him, and Balor laid across his legs, ensuring that his master's dream would not cause him to thrash and possibly injure himself. The dream gave way to another, in which he relived the events in the village. It led to his belief that Brian was someone other than he appeared. However, Brian was not Brian but a giant rat with all the mannerisms and speech patterns of Brian.

Daniel stirred but did not thrash. He awoke just before sunrise and shared his rations with Balor while Macha grazed. Brian woke and whimpered softly through his gag. Daniel knew he could not carry on this neglect too much longer without causing Brian serious injury or even death. He had not fed Brian at all and had only poured drops of water through his gag. Today he would decide Brian's fate. Daniel pondered for a short time and concluded that Brian must die. He removed the cloth that plugged Brian's ears. For the first time in days, Daniel spoke to Brian.

"Hello, Brian."

Brian was slumped over, weak from hunger and thirst, but when he heard Daniel's voice he sat up in disbelief. He turned his head toward the source of the voice even though he could not see. He moved his head back and forth in disbelief.

"Calm down. I am going to ask a few questions. Nod for yes and shake your head for no. Do you understand?"

Brian nodded.

"Good. Now, I want to remove your binds and blindfold, but I do not want you to speak or cry out. Do you understand?"

Brian hesitated for a few moments before responding. He had his own questions, but he struggled to comprehend this strange twist to his current situation. Why did Daniel not free him immediately? Why did he hesitate and ask these questions first? Brian was not in any position to resist, so he nodded once again.

"Excellent. Blindfold first."

Daniel cut away the blindfold, and Brian opened his eyes. He quickly shut them from the sudden onslaught of light that had been absent all this time. He squinted and opened his eyes little by little to allow his vision to adjust. His vision was blurred, and it took some time for it to clear. Before him, Daniel squatted with the huge dog by his side. Brian's eyes widened when he realized that Daniel was unharmed.

"Relax, Brian. I'm going to remove your gag. Remember, do not speak."

Brian nodded. As Daniel's hands moved toward him, he shrunk back instinctively. Daniel moved closer and supported his head with one hand while he removed the gag with the other. It was filthy and emitted a pungent odor from being in Brian's mouth so long. Brian attempted to speak. Even though his mouth formed the words, a weak, raspy cough was all he could muster. Brian's mouth, tongue, and throat felt as if he had been fed sawdust. Daniel offered Brian some water, and Brian opened his mouth to receive the life-giving fluid. Daniel permitted him to have only a few sips. He knew that too much water too soon would cause Brian to vomit.

"Now, most importantly, I'm going to cut away your binds. Just sit and relax. I will answer all your questions in due time. Understood?"

Brian looked into Daniel's eyes and saw that they revealed nothing, but he still felt uneasy, as if something terrible was about to happen. Although he was weak, he still preferred to be free from his bondage rather than tied. He nodded. Daniel cut his binds, and Brian rubbed his wrists. They were sore and raw.

Daniel broke off some bread and handed it to Brian. Brian was tempted to gobble up the chunk of bread but knew his fate if he did so. With great discipline, he took small bites and chewed several times before swallowing. He followed each bite of bread with a swallow of water. Brian felt his strength slowly return. Daniel rose out of his squat and moved several feet away.

Brian sat against the tree he had previously been tied to and stretched out his legs. His muscles were tight and cramped. He needed time and sustenance to get back to full strength. This could take several hours or even days. He finished his bread and continued to take sips from the water skin. After a while, he looked up and was about to speak.

"I said no talking!" Daniel reminded him.

Brian closed his mouth.

"Now, I'm sure you have many questions. What happened that one morning? Why? Who captured you? How can I still be alive? Where were we, and where are we going?"

Brian nodded after each, and Daniel chuckled. His chuckling frightened Brian. A knot formed in his stomach.

Daniel continued, "You, sir, are very good. You serve your master well."

Brian felt as though he was being accused of something and did not like where this inquisition was leading. He could not hold his tongue any longer.

"What are you talking about?"

Balor growled and stepped toward Brian. The dog was so close to Brian that he could smell the dog's breath. Drool seeped out of Balor's mouth, grew heavy, and broke from his lip. It splashed onto Brian's right boot. Brian quickly shrunk back against the trunk of the tree.

"*Silence!* I will give you an opportunity to speak your piece before God. I will answer your questions. Do you think I'm stupid or ignorant? *Do you?*"

Brian shook his head.

"You don't think I knew what you were doing each night? You may have been hunting for dinner, but you were also leaving subtle trail markers behind so your master's henchmen could follow us."

Brian shook his head again. "No, I was—"

Daniel was furious now. He bounded across the distance between him and Brian and snatched him up to his feet by his hair. Brian's eyes teared up from the pain and fear of what could happen to him if he continued to anger the knight.

"And too many questions ... my *friend*," Daniel continued sarcastically as his left hand moved to Brian's throat.

It grew more and more difficult for Brian to breathe. His breath came in short, panicked gasps. As his cheeks turned from pink to red to a shade of purple, Brian's eyes began to bulge and tear up. Daniel peered deep into those eyes and saw the life slowly fade. Everything around Daniel slowed to almost a standstill. It was as if he had been removed from time and space. He was in the tree branches above, looking down at himself as he choked the life out of Brian. While in the tree, Daniel witnessed a child tug on his tunic below, the same child who had helped him back in the village. Daniel was not in the tree anymore but staring into Brian's eyes as they slowly rolled back into his head. Daniel eased his grip as he looked down to see who pulled on his tunic.

No one was there. Brian slumped to the ground on all fours and gasped for air. Daniel looked around. There was no child to be found. Macha and Balor did not seem shaken by the sudden appearance and disappearance of the child. Confused and angered, but not to the point that he wanted to kill—no, murder—Brian, Daniel turned away from Brian and walked toward his two companions. He did not know whom he was angry at anymore.

Balor and Macha recognized the look in their master's eyes and knew that whomever Daniel released his rage on would most likely die. Daniel turned and went back toward Brian, who looked up and pleaded for his life.

"Please, please, don't torture me. Don't kill me. I know where she is."

Daniel stopped dead in his tracks. He was stunned by what he heard.

"What? Who?"

"The witch … I mean, her." Brian caught himself as he realized that calling the knight's love a witch would only infuriate him beyond any boundary.

Daniel snatched him up and shook him like a rag doll.

"What do you mean you know where she is?"

"I know where she was taken."

Daniel gave two short whistles, and both of his companions moved closer to take up guard positions on Brian. Daniel walked into the forest and returned several minutes later with flower petals, roots, and mushrooms. He went to Macha and removed a small wooden bowl from his pack. Daniel pulled the petals into small pieces, shaved the roots, and sliced the mushrooms into the bowl. He turned the knife around and began to use the hilt as a pestle. The process of mashing the contents of the makeshift mortar into a pulp took several minutes. Brian looked on, confused, and began to panic as his thoughts wandered to the extreme end of paranoia.

Is he going to poison me? Poison makes for such a painful death. Just run me through with your sword!

Brian's breaths were short and quick. Beads of sweat formed on his forehead. Daniel mumbled to himself as he picked up the wineskins and water skins. He did not taste test each; instead, he poured the contents onto his palm. Daniel turned his palm over each time the liquid failed the test. Finally, Daniel looked at Brian, shrugged his shoulders, and spoke to himself.

"It's not perfect, but it will have to do."

Daniel approached Brian with the bowl in one hand and a water skin in the other. He had sheathed his blade. Macha and Balor stepped aside as Daniel knelt down and faced Brian. He poured a small amount of the water into the mixture.

"Sir, what is that mixture?"

"This, my friend, is a truth remedy. With this it is impossible to lie."

"Um, I'm telling the truth. And anyway, I'm not hungry or thirsty."

"You leave me no choice. You always know exactly what to say at the right time. I was about to choke the life out of your worthless body when you told me you knew what happened to her. I don't believe in coincidence. I am running out of time, so when you take this, I will ask a series of questions that you will answer. If I do not like the responses—well, let's just say that the wolves will eat tonight."

Brian pleaded for his life again, this time on his knees as he tried to cover his mouth with both. Daniel kicked him in his chest, and Brian toppled over in a heap, weeping.

Daniel pressed his knee onto Brian's chest, forcing him to cry out and, thus, open his mouth. Daniel held his head still and brought the bowl to Brian's lips. With just a little more pressure on Brian's chest, his mouth would open wide enough for Daniel to pour the contents down his throat. Daniel peered into Brian's eyes, and Brian looked back at Daniel—no, not back at Daniel. He looked past the knight. Daniel suddenly dropped the bowl, spilling the contents on the ground beside Brian. Daniel's face grimaced, his eyes closed, and he collapsed with all of his weight onto Brian.

The voices seemed so far away, hundreds of miles away. How could Daniel hear voices so far away? The voices gained clarity, but he did not want to make sense of them. His head screamed in pain. A warm, loving hand cradled his head as another gentle hand patted it down with a cool, wet rag. The rag smelled of the village market on a crowded, hot, summer day. He moaned and reached for the place from which the pain emanated. As Daniel touched it, he winced in pain and squeezed his eyes shut. He had no idea what had happened. One moment, he was about to empty the contents of the bowl down Brian's throat, and the next—blackness.

Daniel eased his eyes open slowly. The rays of the sun disoriented his vision. "What happened?"

A familiar voice—close, soft, and encouraging—answered Daniel, "I apologize, Toad, if I injured you, but in your anger, the mixture you attempted to force your companion to drink would not have had the effect you sought."

Daniel moaned as he sat up. He took the cold compress from the monk's hand and applied it to the back of his head. As he opened his eyes fully, he noticed a hand-sized rock on the ground by his side with some blood on it. He reasoned the blood belonged to him.

"Athair, what are you talking about? How did you know what I was attempting to do? And with the knowledge of nature you have at your disposal, you chose to hit me on the back of the head with a rock?"

"Mac, I may have hit you harder than previously thought. You know the answers to all the questions you asked, but I shall attempt to clarify while you nurse your injury. First, you know I am fully aware of everything you do, particularly when your physical presence is in close proximity to mine. Second, you sought me out for answers, and when I did not give you the responses you expected, even though I did answer your questions, you looked elsewhere for the answers. The closest person you sought for answers was your companion here, whom you almost murdered. Yes, murdered. I observed you gather the ingredients you needed to extract the truth from your friend—"

"Athair, he is not my friend, or my companion." The monk smacked Daniel on the top of the head. Daniel flinched in pain, and Brian chuckled. Daniel looked at Brian with anger.

"Do not interrupt!" The monk continued, "As you gathered the ingredients, it was quite evident that you were in a rage. It took you a very long time to control your anger, Toad, and yet something your companion said triggered your anger. You went berserk. Although your training and experience kicked in and you knew where and how to gather the ingredients you needed, you still were so angry and desperate for information that you forgot the foremost law of mixtures: *do not deviate* from the ingredients list, the amount of each ingredient, the sequence of the mixture, or the method of combining the ingredients. You failed in all of these, and because of this I could not allow you to commit murder, Toad."

At the mention of murder, Brian fell over unconscious. Daniel held his ground and felt the monk's hand on his shoulder; he turned and did not say anything. He didn't have to. The monk knew how Daniel felt. He could see the shame in his eyes, in his clenched jaw and fists. They were clenched for a fight, not with an external enemy but an internal one, an enemy that Daniel had fought his entire life—his anger. The monk recalled several times when he had witnessed Daniel's anger in full force. It had saved him and Daniel upon several occasions. The monk was well aware of what could happen to the person or persons who caused his anger.

Daniel turned and knelt in front of the one person who knew him better than himself, Athair. The monk knelt across from Daniel and asked, "What is troubling you, Mac? Why have you gone from the path of righteousness?"

"Athair, you should know why. You told me you knew I was coming to you."

"Although true I knew you were coming to me, I do not know the why."

Daniel hung his head as he related in explicit detail all the events and occurrences leading up to his "attempted murder" of Brian. The entire episode took longer than fifteen minutes due to Daniel's having to restrain his anger several times. Each time, the monk provided comfort and reassurance by placing his right hand on Daniel's shoulder.

"I am fine now, Athair. Thank you. Now, do you understand why I must continue my quest?"

"I do, Mac, but you are not fine. You lost control. If it were not for me, you would have killed that man and set out on a course that would have been almost impossible to return from."

Daniel soaked in the monk's words as he remembered the years he had spent with him. He had arrived mistakenly upon the old man's small hut, or at least Daniel thought it was a mistake. The old man sheltered him and taught him the ways of the natural world, as well as the ancient manners. It took Daniel several years as a pupil to learn and understand that Athair did not force Daniel to subdue his emotions, especially his anger. Athair taught Daniel how to control his emotions and use them. He learned that emotions are a part of him and that, when controlled, they can be most beneficial, sometimes life-saving. However, Daniel also learned that when emotions controlled him, there were few benefits. Uncontrolled emotions could prove dangerous and deadly to those around him.

"Mac, you cannot go on this trek alone. There is too much at stake."

"I know—Cassandra."

"I was not speaking about her."

Brian stirred. Daniel stood up slowly. He seemed to have recovered from the blow to his head. He approached Brian and reached for him with both hands—huge, muscular hands that the monk had witnessed crushing the windpipes of men bigger than the knight himself. The monk moved quickly, raised his arm, and prepared to give a nonlethal blow to his head. Daniel reached closer for Brian, grabbed his shoulders, and lifted him to his feet.

"Athair, I felt you move toward me," Daniel said, still gripping Brian.

"Yes, but you still cannot go on this trek alone."

"I'm going home," Brian muttered.

Daniel released Brian. The monk walked toward Brian. Daniel moved toward Macha as Balor fell in on his left side.

CHAPTER 10

The monk reached into his robe. He produced a root and gave it Brian to chew on. Daniel recognized it but could not put a name to it. Healers gave it to those who had suffered a shocking experience to help them regain their strength and orientation. "Rescued from death" qualified. Athair led Brian away from Daniel to a tree about thirty yards away, out of earshot of Daniel, who could only see Athair's back but observed Brian's nods. As Athair and Brian continued their discourse, Daniel got ready to continue his mission. He adjusted Macha's saddle, gave Balor some of his rations, secured his weapons, and mounted.

Athair raised his hand and drew Daniel's attention. As much as Daniel felt the urge to leave, he remained and waited. He respected and loved the monk, and he could not act hastily. Daniel sat for a few minutes while Athair finished with Brian. They both turned and walked toward Daniel. Brian appeared in a much more jovial mood.

"I have changed my mind. I am going with you," Brian stated.

"I do not need anyone. I will find her on my own."

"On the contrary, Toad. You need us," the monk retorted.

Daniel looked down at the monk, and Brian shifted his gaze from one to the other.

"Why?"

"I have all the information you need," Brian replied.

"And I am the only one who can bring you back to the path," added Athair.

After several moments of deliberation, Daniel shrugged. "You both are correct. There are enemy forces everywhere, and in my current mental state I may not be able to discern friend from foe. As much as I hate to admit it, I do need both of you. Brian, if Athair says you are a friend, then I must believe him."

"Toad, he is a friend. Perhaps the strongest ally you have other than myself. You will see."

"Let us go then! We have much time and distance to make up."

Daniel turned Macha, and the two companions walked alongside.

"This is not going to work," he said after a short while. "Not only will you both be unable to keep up, but we will lose valuable time and distance walking. We need to get both of you horses."

"Agreed," the monk said.

"I know of a town not far from here where we should be able to appropriate—I mean, obtain—some horses," Brian offered.

Daniel and Athair looked at Brian. Daniel dismounted so he could also walk.

"Brian, no stealing," Athair chided.

"Who said anything about stealing? All I said was we can get some horses in a nearby town."

"It's how you said it and the words you used. Unfortunately, we do not have enough to purchase two horses so we will certainly have to figure out a way …"

Before Daniel finished his thought, and as the party cleared a bend in the road, they observed a couple (a man and a woman with an infant) being accosted by five highwaymen. All were on foot and armed. It was obvious that this point in the road provided a perfect location for unwary travelers to be harassed by the denizens of the forest. But this seemed to be an atypical robbery. These particular ruffians had their weapons drawn on an unarmed family and looked for more than money. Four of them stood approximately the same height and build, and all wore leather. The fifth, the leader, was taller, was better dressed, and directed the action without any weapons in his hands. They all had daggers sheathed at the waist, but all carried different weapons. Two robbers, one armed with a mace and the other a short sword, pulled the man and woman out of their saddles and onto the ground. The infant screamed hysterically as the mother almost dropped it. Daniel and Brian drew their weapons and Balor growled, but a snap of Daniel's fingers silenced him. The highwaymen failed to notice them, and since they were outnumbered, Daniel did not want to lose the advantage of surprise. If Athair was nervous or stressed, he did not show it. Two of the ruffians, armed with a staff and a halberd, split up. They positioned themselves on either side of the site to observe up and down the road to provide security. Daniel realized it was only a matter of seconds before his huge frame atop Macha would cause the one with the halberd to sound the alarm. Two clicks of Daniel's tongue against the back of his teeth gave Balor and Macha the opportunity they had trained for and lived many times. Balor took off into the edge of the forest with the intent to circle around and attack the backs of the enemy, while Daniel on top of Macha bolted straight into battle, creating the diversion.

Brian tried to keep up but only maintained a steady pace. Athair silently ran alongside Brian without making a sound. For a very old man, Athair was in phenomenal condition. The robber with the halberd sounded the alarm. The leader drew his sword and pointed it at the infant, and the ruffian with the mace clubbed the father to eliminate any immediate threat. The halberd- and staff-bearing robbers disappeared briefly into the edge of the forest only to reappear with five archers armed with short bows and arrows fitted and pointing at the party. When Daniel reined in Macha, the archers spread out to form a complete circle. Brian and Athair caught up to Daniel and Macha and stood on either side of them.

"No one move," Daniel said and then made three clicks, but the attack from Balor did not come. "Athair, you are so right. I am not thinking clearly. I should have realized that ordinary highwaymen would not have an assortment of weapons normally used by the guards of a city or abbey."

The leader advanced to stand among the archers. He stared down Daniel and the rest of his party.

"The world-renowned Opal Knight taken by a clever ruse," the leader mocked as he gestured toward Daniel. He continued, "I told the farmer that I could capture him."

Several of the band quickly disarmed Daniel and Brian. They searched Athair but found no weapons. The monk did not appear to need any. Brian sweated profusely. Daniel's breathing became heavy, and his face flushed with anger. Athair whispered something to Daniel, and the redness began to fade slowly.

"Ensure their bindings are tight, especially the knight's. I don't know anything about the other two, but stories and legends tell of this knight possessing ancient knowledge that allows him to perform inhuman feats."

The guards finished tying the bindings and ensured

that Daniel's were tighter than the others. The three were then tied together by a rope around each of their necks, a common treatment of prisoners after a battle. Athair looked at Daniel and saw the look of concern in his eyes. Daniel knew that if they did not act before being imprisoned, their chance of escape would fade to nothing, and, worse for Daniel, Cassandra's would diminish as well.

"Sir," one of the guards reported, "the prisoners are ready for transport. What do we do with the family?" The guard pointed to the family that was besieged earlier.

"Kill them. They are of no use to us anymore."

Half of the archers turned toward the family. Daniel's mind spun as he tried to absorb everything that had happened since Athair joined the party.

The father raised his hands in defiance. But instead of speaking in defiance, he appealed for mercy. "Wait, please, kind sir. We did as you asked. We won't say anything. We don't even know who the Opal Knight is or what he has done to deserve the fate that awaits him."

At this request, the archers lowered their bows. Perhaps they realized that killing unarmed citizens was an act of murder and not mercy. Maybe they didn't know what the father referred to. Either way, the leader had a dilemma. If all of the guards had not looked to the leader earlier, now they at least focused their hearing on his next words.

"Typical. It has always amazed me what will come out of people's mouths when faced with the impending moment of death," the leader stated coolly. "I'm feeling quite generous today. Bind the family too. Their lives are spared but not their freedom."

"Wait. What are you going to do with us?" the mother asked.

"Well, your husband will go to prison with the rest. You will fetch a fair price on the slave market, and your baby will be raised as a soldier."

"*No!*"

The mother lunged but was quickly restrained and bound with everyone else. Two guards hesitated, but a look from the leader woke them from their daze. Last checks of the prisoners were made, and the party moved off. The guards tried to secure Macha, but she bolted into the forest, and the leader decided that chasing after a dumb animal was a waste of time.

The entire group, guards and prisoners, walked for about an hour before arriving at the edge of a town. The leader gave the order, and the guards changed into their uniforms, which would show from where their authority came. The guards dressed like most town constabulary, but each town had its signature tunic. Daniel waited to see their tunics to ascertain some clue as to the identity of the farmer, but he was disappointed. This leader was far too clever. Obviously, the guards were well trained and under orders not to give away their true identity. Their uniforms minus the tunic were enough to give the leader any authority he needed.

The guards tied the prisoners to a large oak. They were positioned sitting cross-legged with about a foot between their shoulders. Two guards remained in charge of the prisoners, while the others circled the leader for final instructions. The sentries stepped off to be within earshot of the meeting. This allowed Daniel to gain some insight as to exactly what had occurred.

Daniel whispered to the mother, who was tied to him on his left side. He could listen and observe the sentries this way.

"My name is Daniel. Why did you and your husband trick us into being captured?"

The woman sobbed. She turned toward Daniel and said, "We … I am sorry. We are pilgrims traveling to the grave site of the one who drove out the snakes. These soldiers, guards, or whatever they are stopped us. The one in charge told us that he needed our help in the capture of an evil man. We were hesitant at first, but he told us many stories of, and, I presume, about you, about how you consorted with and married a witch. He said you were a devil worshipper and sacrificed babies."

"None of that is true."

"We realized that when their leader called you the Opal Knight. We have heard of such a knight. The knight who performed such great, heroic deeds in the service of God could never have done any of the things the leader claimed."

"Never! Someone is keeping me from rescuing my wife. She was kidnapped. But whoever kidnapped her also led me to believe she was killed so I would not pursue her captors. I have no idea who the farmer is, do you? Shh, wait," Daniel whispered as two guards approached, apparently to relieve the first pair of sentries.

The relieved guards moved off to join their companions. One of the new guards took a position facing away from the prisoners so that he was between them and the guard force. The other stealthily moved near the prisoners, avoided Daniel, and knelt near Athair on the opposite side of the tree from Daniel. Shortly, Brian leaned toward Daniel's right shoulder and whispered, "Sir Knight, Athair wants you to listen to the guard."

Daniel nodded, and several seconds later the guard moved from Athair to Daniel. He leaned in and whispered into Daniel's ear.

Daniel nodded as the new sentry whispered, "I knew something was not right about this. My captain never told us who we were after until you happened upon our ruse. The family had no idea what we were doing but agreed to help. When the captain told us to kill the family, I couldn't— we couldn't," and he gestured toward the guard standing between them and the captain.

"Untie us. Give us our weapons, "Daniel demanded.

"Not yet. We won't go into the town until after the sun sets. The captain does not want anyone made suspicious or asking questions about us or the prisoners. Anyway, we still are outnumbered three to one, and outskilled." The guard glanced at the rest of the band tied to the tree. This reminded Daniel that, other than himself, his fighting force consisted of Athair (who could hold his own), Brian (who has some worth), the two guards, a father (who did not appear to have any skill at combat), a woman, and her baby strapped to her bosom. The guard was right. This was neither the time nor the place to make a move at escape or combat.

Daniel nodded. "Do you have a plan?"

"What are you two whispering about? I want to know," demanded Brian.

"Shut up. I will tell you shortly," Daniel stressed through his clenched teeth.

"Yes, I do have a plan." The guard continued, "When we ready to enter the town, I will loosen the monk's bindings, not yours because I believe the captain will make sure yours are secured himself, but I will move the monk into position behind you. After nightfall we will start the march slowly toward town down the road. If the captain deploys us accordingly, he will lead the column flanked by six footmen. Six more will take up positions around all of you, three on each side, leaving the rest to take up the rear. I will be centered and forward of the guards in the rear. I will ensure there is some confusion to distract the guards. This I have not thought of yet, but rest assured you will know the signal. My companion will be in the very rear to draw attention from you. The monk will be able to get out of his binds and free you and the others. Your weapons will be strapped to the horse I will be leading. If all goes according to plan, you should be able to make your way back to the horse and your weapons before the guards on the flank can react."

Daniel nodded his approval of the plan but also formulated one of his own, one slightly different from that of this conspirator. He still had difficulty trusting others. He felt this just might be an excuse for the captain to execute the party on the spot without trial.

Their guards routinely changed until dusk. The prisoners napped except for Daniel. He continued to watch each guard, making mental notes on tendencies, such as which ones were left and right handed, what weapons each preferred to carry, whether any appear to be nursing any recent injuries, and which favored one leg or the other. He was not too concerned about anyone's age. All of them were close to thirty years of age, with three or four in their twenties. The older were certainly more experienced, but what the younger ones lacked in experience they made up in strength, agility, and endurance. All the mental images were crucial intelligence that Daniel would use in the upcoming desperate attempt to escape. Three guards were left handed. He would not know where they deployed in the formation until they formed to depart. This would allow Daniel to quickly determine how to attack. All seemed comfortable with weapons that required a reach: long sword, spear, halberd, battle-ax. This was quite useful information; Daniel and his party would at least have an even chance given that none of those weapons could be immediately deployed for use without injuring, maiming, or even killing fellow guards in close quarters. Daniel also had two weapons that were not considered by anyone, save himself and Athair. Balor and Macha were far enough away to remain out of sight but close enough to quickly respond once Daniel gave the signal.

Dusk soon became darkness, and Daniel's anxiety stirred. Athair murmured some encouraging words to soothe him, but the effect would last only so long. His anxiety did not start to ebb until half the guards lit torches. The welcomed light fought back the darkness that threatened Daniel.

"Stand up!" the captain ordered.

The prisoners attempted to pull one another up but failed. Daniel, Athair, and Brian stood without assistance, and the guards pulled the family up by their shoulders. The baby howled, and Daniel noticed several guards leering at the mother. If they did not escape, she would bear the brunt of the guards' wrath and lust. At last, they all stood. The conspirator placed everyone in line according to the plan he had proposed to Daniel. So far, he had done everything he said he would, but Daniel was still wary.

The party, led by the captain, moved off toward the town. Four of the six guards around the prisoners held torches. Although this made Daniel feel more comfortable, the guards now carried weapons that could be used in close-quarters combat. The party moved off in the direction of the town. The baby was nursed so he no longer cried, but the mother wept noticeably. Her husband attempted to comfort her as much as possible. Brian dragged his feet, and Daniel and Athair remained alert. They all waited for the signal from their collaborator.

CHAPTER 11

he party continued along. The guards were highly experienced with prisoner transport, and although the pace was steady and even, there were no rest breaks for food or water. The Vikings and Crusaders used the same technique to break the will of their prisoners. The Moors, on the other hand, treated prisoners much differently. During the last Crusade, Daniel had been a prisoner and knew that this group of soldiers served the Church.

As they trudged along, the sky grew black, not due to the hour but to dark, low-hanging clouds that rolled in. Flashes of lightning lit the sky. As the thunder grew in intensity, so did the rain. Daniel looked at Athair, who glanced toward their collaborator. The time would be soon. The advantage would be theirs. The guards' footing and close-combat effectiveness would be hampered by the slick, muddy road. Daniel heard a scream from behind and, without looking, knew that was the signal.

The other prisoners looked back while Athair freed Daniel and Brian, who in turn freed the family. A guard behind them was in flames. Apparently, a fellow guard had "accidentally" stumbled into him and lit his tunic with his torch. The fire engulfed him. The stench of burning flesh and clothing filled the air along with thick, black smoke. Brian ran toward the forward guards, Daniel toward the left, and Athair to the right. The smoke, rain, and confusion helped conceal their movement. The father unsheathed the burning guard's short sword and immediately took a defensive posture in front of his wife, who had run toward a huge rock. She crouched near it with her back toward the melee to protect their baby.

The captain shouted orders above the din. The front

guards quickly regrouped and prepared to mount a counterattack. The two collaborators dropped the rear guards one by one. One collaborator rolled away from the thrusts of a halberd and found himself within arm's reach of a severed right hand of one of the guards. It still held a mace. He managed to loosen the death grip around the mace. Now armed with a mace in one hand and a short sword in the other, he fought his way inside the effective radius of the halberd. He easily beat the guard to death with three blows to the head.

As the head of the column readied to counterattack, a huge form leaped from the edge of the forest and crashed into them. Daniel paused to smile as he witnessed Macha rear up on her hind legs. She stomped and flailed her front legs like two huge maces in rhythm. First, she struck down four guards one by one, and then she trampled them to death. Daniel moved from one guard to another, striking them down, while Brian and Athair did their part to protect his rear. At Daniel's signal, Brian and Athair fought their way toward the family at the huge rock to assist the father in protecting his wife and child. The father was appalled that they had abandoned the Opal Knight.

"How could you leave him? He is outnumbered. It's an unfair fight!"

Athair calmly remarked, "You, sir, obviously, have never witnessed a Templar Knight in battle. He may be outnumbered, but it is only an unfair fight for his opponents. Watch."

A guard lunged at Athair and the others with a halberd. Athair stepped deftly aside, and as the halberd missed its intentional target, it found another.

The captain rallied five guards to him and surrounded Daniel. The captain limped, injured by one of Macha's huge hooves. Daniel dropped his shield and picked up another short sword. Now armed with two short swords, he had two perfect weapons for close-quarters combat. However, the guards still had the advantage. They hesitated to advance any further after witnessing what Daniel had done to their companions. The two collaborators still held their own with the remainder of the guards who had chosen them as targets. They could not disengage or assist Daniel.

Daniel stood his ground and breathed deeply. He slowly turned to gain any insight into any of the guards' tendencies and weaknesses. By now, all of the guards had substituted their long-shafted weapons for those more suitable for close-quarters combat. Most had short swords, with two holding maces. The captain stood to the outside of the circle and utilized hand and arm signals to direct the attack. Daniel took both of his swords and stuck them into the ground with the hilts up. Confused, the circle of guards delayed their attack.

Daniel knelt. He heard a scream and then another from the rock where the family had taken refuge. Neither sounded like a woman's scream, so he could only surmise that Athair, Brian, and the father had dispatched the guards who had attacked the family. Daniel stretched out his arms and looked to the heavens in prayer. He closed his eyes. The guards looked at each other. Most had never seen this type of behavior from an opponent and did not know how to react.

But the Captain had had enough of Daniel's nonsense.

Through clenched teeth and with a hoarse voice, he relayed a simple command: "Kill him!"

As the guards stepped forward at the command, Balor ran through the tall grass and knocked over the captain. Like a lion severing the windpipe of a gazelle, Balor's canines found their mark. The captain's life spurted out in red as his heart pumped frantically until he died.

Daniel jumped to his feet, grasped both swords, and swung them in unison. One sword deflected and parried while the other sliced through flesh, cartilage, and bone. He dropped each guard until he alone stood at the center of the circle. He breathed heavily as he turned and watched his collaborators finish their opponents. The entire guard force lay dead. Macha and Balor walked from opposite ends of the battleground toward their master. They surveyed the battle area for any more threats. Seeing none, they resumed their short walk toward their master.

"My friends, you performed superbly," Daniel said, hugging each, "and neither of you are injured."

A voice from the rock blurted, "I wish that was true for all of us."

Daniel turned toward the voice. As his anger subsided, aided by the hugs and affection from Macha and Balor, Daniel recognized Brian's voice. By now Athair, Brian, and the two collaborators formed a circle that obstructed Daniel's view of the victim inside. As Daniel approached, he heard the baby crying. That meant one thing: this baby would grow up with one parent less. Life was difficult as it is, never mind without one parent. Images flashed through Daniel's mind of life for this fatherless or motherless child.

A motherless life might be somewhat easier. The father

could easily find another woman to marry and care for the child. The Church did not view remarrying due to a spouse's death as a sin, so the child would not be excommunicated as a bastard. A fatherless life, however, was an entirely different existence. And it was an existence, not a life. No man would marry a widow with a child. The child and mother would live as outcasts on the periphery of a village, subsisting only on the kindness of the villagers.

Daniel pushed Brian aside and entered the circle. What he observed was not one of the options that had run through his mind only a few minutes earlier. Lying on the ground on his back was the baby, covered in blood. He cried uncontrollably. How could so much blood come from such a small innocent? The baby should be dead. But the blood did not belong to the baby. Daniel's gaze shifted and traced the puddle of blood to its source. The blood had pooled under the baby on level ground. A thin stream of red flowed from the large rock face. Daniel slowly lifted his eyes and followed the thin stream backward to its source. His eyes fell upon four feet. Two were firmly planted, and two others faced inward so that all four booted feet pointed toward each other and touched. Daniel looked up and saw the lance that had pierced the baby's mother through her back and penetrated her right lung. The lance continued its path into the father's chest and heart. The father hugged his wife—the last embrace the two gave each other. Apparently, a guard had raced up the hill toward the outcropping and managed to penetrate the defense of Athair and Brian. By instinct alone, and without any regard for her life, the mother turned with child in hand and managed to lift the baby high in order to keep him from being skewered also.

The iron tip of the lance wedged in a crack behind the father. The lance held the parents in a final, loving embrace. They had watched the life fade from each other's eyes.

Athair reached down, picked up the baby, and cleaned him with the hem of his robe. This soothed the infant. Brian and the collaborators took to the task of burying the parents of the now-orphaned child.

Daniel moved toward the collaborators. "You two fought bravely. We were skeptical, but you proved yourself. More importantly you proved yourself worthy of my friendship and loyalty. What are your names?"

"Michael and John."

Daniel extended his right arm to each and in turn grasped each one's forearm, thus consummating the ritual of acceptance and friendship. Michael was the tall, bearded one, while James was several inches shorter and broader. However, the facial resemblance, mannerisms, and accents gave it away that these two were brothers.

John, Michael, and Brian moved the bodies of the parents to a remote area behind the rock outcrop and buried them together. Brian beckoned Daniel over.

"Sir, they were Christian and deserve a Christian burial," he stated, looking at Daniel.

Although Daniel realized they still had to dispose of the remaining bodies and get back on track to rescue Cassandra, a representative of the Church had to preside over the burial to ensure that the departed souls received absolution and aid in their travel to Paradise. Daniel knew he was the closest of the party to represent the Church. He had studied for many years under the tutelage of an abbey and was, in fact, a Templar.

The graveside service was short and concise, but Daniel's words stayed with the party forever: "Lord, we gather together in Your presence to humbly request that You receive Your two children into Your heart. Their love for each other knew no bounds, except for the love of their only child. It was a love as great as that of Your Son, who gave His life to save all of ours. These two humble servants gave both of their lives to save their only son. Comfort them as You receive them into Your home. Console them with the knowledge that their child will be cared for by all of us. We pray this in Your name. Amen."

The party collectively echoed "Amen." Daniel moved away to finish the disposal of the other bodies. Athair, Brian, John, and Michael looked at one another.

Finally, Brian broke the silence. "What exactly did he mean that we would care for the child?"

"Exactly that, Brian," Athair confirmed. "The child is our responsibility now."

"Get moving! I can't hide all of these bodies myself!" Daniel turned and yelled to the mourners.

The group moved toward Daniel with Brian in the lead and John and Michael on either side of Athair, who still held the baby.

"He's going to need a name, you know," John mentioned out loud.

"True," Michael replied

"You two are babbling as if this is a done deal. The knight made a decision—a life-changing decision—for all of us without even consulting us. Doesn't that bother any of you?" Brian interjected.

"It doesn't bother me," John answered. "What about you, Michael?"

"I'm fine with it."

"And you, monk?"

"Fate wields her hand once more."

"So all three of you are okay with someone else determining what you do next?" Brian was rather annoyed by the group's passivity.

John spoke up, "Michael and I have trained practically our entire lives to soldier. We volunteered when the militia went through the town on its annual recruitment. We were raised by a father who was the captain of the guard, so being told what to do by a leader, in this instance, the knight, is quite natural for us and accepting."

"That makes sense, but you both clearly disobeyed your captain's orders. So that argument has no merit."

Michael spoke this time. "No merit? Those orders from the captain were immoral and violated our code of honor. Once that captain issued those commands, we were no longer bound to obey or serve him. This infant is an orphan now. What would you think we should do? Leave him for the wolves? No, we shall not. We would be just as guilty of murder as the captain is. Our souls would be damned. The baby is innocent. We must protect him until we find a suitable home for him."

By this time, the group had arrived to where Daniel had dragged the bodies into the high grass. Athair sat against a tall pine with the baby asleep in his arms. The infant seemed at peace in his arms, and this amazed Brian and the brothers. Balor sat near Athair while Macha roamed nearby grazing, but her ears were ever twitching, ever alert. The four hid the bodies deep in the tall, thick grass. They left the bodies clothed but removed all the weapons, armor, and anything else that might identify them as professional military. To a casual passerby, it would seem they were the victims of a large band of brigands. To a professional, it would seem just as it was—professional soldiers ambushed and killed by a superior force. Either way, the bodies would not be discovered for several days, more than enough time for the group to add distance between them and their pursuers.

It rained again, and the party quickly gathered what each could comfortably carry. They distributed the weapons, money, and armor evenly. Daniel and Athair did not accept any of the booty. They buried anything that could not be carried. Speed was of the essence, and extra weight would slow them down just as much as the infant.

"Toad, the child will need milk. I can keep him pacified and calm for only so long. It will only be a matter of time before hunger and the need for nourishment will overpower the containment I have over him," Athair reported.

Daniel nodded and called the group together for a conference.

The group gathered in a small circle and knelt around Athair and the infant. Every other member faced out for security. As Daniel composed himself, Brian spoke up.

"Sir Knight, the others and I have been talking about how we didn't think it was fair of you to make the decision for all of us regarding the baby."

John and Michael looked dumbfounded, and Athair just gently shook his head in disbelief.

Daniel paused. He opened and closed his fists. "Is that true?" he asked the brothers.

"Of course not. He lies!" Michael retorted.

"Ask the monk!" Brian demanded.

"I have no need to ask Athair. I know his answer. The brothers are devout Christians and would never permit an innocent child to be left behind for dead. You are the only one who has taken issue with my decision. Brian, we have been through a lot in a short amount of time, and by now you must know how I feel about those who cannot defend themselves. I have always protected the less fortunate. If you still do not wish to save a life, then you are more than welcome to leave, but if you decide to stay, you must be committed to the safety and protection of the child."

"Dammit! Sir Knight, I have almost been killed more times in the past few days than in my entire life," Brian began with disdain, "one time by *you*! I can't do this anymore. This journey gets more and more dangerous each day, and I get farther away from home. It seems every time we get closer to finding the wit—I mean, your wife—something distracts us from the task. When will it end?"

"It ends when I say it ends." Daniel stood up, looked Brian in the eye, and waited for a decision.

Brian stretched out his right hand. "Farewell. It has been dangerous, but it certainly was a lot safer than waking the wife after a few pints."

Daniel lifted his hand to bid Brian farewell, but he dropped it quickly without grasping Brian's hand.

"What did you just say?"

"Dammit! Which part? You almost killing me or the part about being safer with the wife?"

"No, the part about Cassandra."

"You mean, every time we get close to finding her something distracts us?

"That's it! Brian, you are a genius!"

"Well, I don't know about genius, but I am very smart … wait, what are you talking about? A few minutes ago you were getting ready to send me on my way, and now I'm a genius?" Brian asked, confused.

"Distractions. The key is distractions," the Opal Knight began. "Athair, Brian, think about it. Every time we moved closer to finding some much-needed information or intelligence regarding Cassandra, something has distracted us. Reflect. My abduction and escape from the abbey; being chased underground with Brian; our pursuit through the forest; my attempted murder of you, Brian; and now, this infant. All have happened during this campaign."

Athair handed the infant to John. "Yes, yes, it all makes sense now. I am getting old. I should have recognized what was happening. There is a perturbation."

"What are you two talking about? Who is Cassandra?" Michael asked.

"We must stay the course. We must find her!" Daniel demanded.

Daniel and Athair moved away from the rest of the party. Brian leaned in toward John and Michael and brought them up to date on the events thus far. The brothers did not seem happy that they had been duped into the capture of the Opal Knight and his companions or with their current situation. Daniel and Athair returned. Focused and energized, they knew what they were truly up against. John and Michael held their own conference.

Daniel quickly gave the order to depart. Athair

approached John and reached for the infant, but he did not hand the baby over.

"Sir Knight, my brother and I have discussed the present situation, and we do not think that the trek you are on is any place for an orphaned infant."

"It certainly is not," the knight agreed, "but what other choices are there?"

"Very few," John continued, "but the one choice that is most beneficial and safest for the child is for us—Michael, myself, and the infant—to part ways with you. We know of an orphanage to the south near Cork that will ensure the child receives the best of care. Someone may even adopt him and care for him as if he were their own."

Daniel was taken aback. "There must be a better way. You two are excellent fighters and tacticians. Your knowledge of the inner workings of the local governments and militia will benefit us greatly."

"Thank you for your kind words, but we are still somewhat shaken by the lies told to us by the captain. We need time to ourselves and will seek out a priest for the absolution of our sins."

"Yes, but—" Daniel was cut short by a tug on his arm from Athair.

"Toad, this is what we were just referring to. The infant, like it or not, is a distraction. This is the best course of action for all involved. We can continue to head east toward the coast, and the brothers will head south with the infant."

"True. We will not hold you any longer. Once the child is safe, you are welcome to rejoin us at the Dublin harbor. We will be there in three days."

The party split exactly in half. John and Michael headed

south with the infant, while Daniel, Brian, and Athair turned east toward Dublin. All were on horseback because they were able to secure the horses from their former captors. The other horses that survived were relieved of their armor and tack and set free. Daniel assumed they would make their way to town and be rounded up. Perhaps they would start a wild herd.

Daniel pressed the pace; he wanted to get as far away from the carnage as possible before nightfall. The three, along with Balor and Macha, made it to a hilltop that overlooked the town below and the road south. They watched John and Michael get smaller and smaller as the distance between the two parties grew.

"They are good men," Athair stated.

"Yes, they are. I fear for their safety."

"They left *us*. We are the ones in danger. Why do you fear for their safety?" Brian asked.

"That may be true, Brian, but eventually, it will become known that they aided in the escape of three fugitives from the Church. Additionally, they corroborated in the killing of soldiers under the protection of the Church. For those two acts alone, a price will be on their heads as steep as the one on ours."

With that last dose of reality, Daniel pulled on Macha's reins to the right and led Athair and Brian deep into the forest. They traveled each day until dusk and built the usual large fire with Balor and Macha taking their positions. Each of the three also stood guard while the other two slept. Two days and nights passed without incident. On the morning of the third day, Daniel told the others to wait and get ready to move out while he scouted ahead. It had not been that long ago that Daniel had traveled the same route toward Galway upon his return from the most recent Crusade to the Holy Land. Daniel moved to the edge of the forest and walked toward Dublin, the largest city in Ireland. He loved Ireland, but Dublin was much too busy for his taste. However, in order to become someone in this world, understanding city life was a necessity. As he entered the open gates, he wondered how John and Michael had fared. He had grown to genuinely respect those brothers.

CHAPTER 12

ichael and John made their way south toward Cork, one of the major cities of Ireland. Not too much earlier, five or six years perhaps, the entire Cork population had almost been wiped out by the Black Death. As a major port of entry for shipping, it was only a matter of time before the Black Death visited the city. The Black Death caused painful swelling around the ears, in the throat, under the arms, and around the groin. Chills and fever soon followed, accompanied by headaches, weakness throughout the body, abdominal pain, vomiting, diarrhea, chest pain, and coughing. The tissue bled and died, giving the appearance of the skin becoming blackened—hence the name Black Death.

The trek toward Cork would take at least one week, but the brothers knew of a village within two days' walk where the Dominican monks often took in and sheltered orphans. Due to its proximity of the village to Cork, Michael and John knew they would not be harassed by any soldiers. Fear of contracting the Black Death saw to that.

As they neared the village, John remained hidden with the baby while Michael approached the village to ensure they would not walk into a trap. Michael conducted reconnaissance, and it was lucky that he did. In addition to the usual conglomerate of merchants, tavern goers, and townspeople, a small contingent of soldiers was present. Michael entered the tavern and ordered mead.

While in the tavern, he did not gather much information other than what he already knew. Most of the chatter centered around rumors of the Black Death and its famous victims, none of whom Michael had heard of, but he supposed every community had its heroes and villains. He discovered one interesting fact when two soldiers entered the tavern and sat down near him. Initially, Michael thought the soldiers recognized him or were suspicious, but it turned out they were just trying to find a seat to relax after a long day on patrol. The two looked very different from the soldiers farther north. Both had prominent Norse features, an influence from the invasions.

"Timothy, I thought the day would never end," one said.

"Aye, Dennis. Any word on when we will be leaving this hole in the ground and return to Dublin?"

Michael drank and avoided eye contact. Eye contact from a stranger in a place like this would appear as a challenge, and he was not in any position to take on two highly trained soldiers—not that he didn't think he had a good chance of success. But the melee would draw more soldiers to the scene. He would be arrested, questioned, and tortured, not necessarily in that order. So he remained as uncaring as possible and appeared only interested in finding the bottom of his mug only to refill it again.

Dennis responded, glancing only briefly at the stranger across from them. "Our force was sent here in case those fugitives thought about turning south. The captain should have captured them by now. Certainly he is headed toward Dublin with them. It would only be a matter of time before that Templar would be before His Eminence in France."

Michael did not recognize these soldiers, but they knew of his captain and of their mission. In such a short period of time, these two soldiers unknowingly answered many questions for Michael. He had to get to John quickly. They had a higher calling now. Michael got up to leave, but in his haste he bumped the table and spilled the two soldiers' drinks. Timothy jumped to his feet, prepared to move toward Michael. Dennis grabbed Timothy by his arm.

"Brother, it's not worth the trouble. Anyway, it was an accident and we are off duty."

Dennis sat down and turned his attention back toward what was left of his drink. As a show of good faith, Michael ordered a round for the soldiers, paid his tab, and exited the tavern. He located the church and the monks' quarters. There was a suitable location to leave the infant that would guarantee the child's safety until his discovery in the morning. Michael continued his nonchalant way around the village until he made his way back out of the town. He then moved deliberately toward John's hiding position. His path ensured that he could double back without raising suspicion to see if he was followed. No one followed Michael, and he soon arrived to John and the infant. Michael fed the infant some milk he had acquired from a lone goat staked out in a pen. He relayed to John what he had learned. John had several questions. Michael pointed out that it was getting dark and that they would have to make their way toward the village and the monks' quarters to leave the child.

"John, we have to stay sharp and focused on the task at hand. Once we deliver the child, I will answer your questions."

The full moon provided sufficient light as they made their way toward the village.

Daniel joined the throng of people who moved in and out of the city gates. One thing about a city that was the center of civilization for a nation is that the different classes of society intermingled. A definite separation of classes existed, most noticeable by the different types of garb worn. The nobles almost always rode horseback, and as much as they wanted to push their way through the city gates to establish their place in society, the horde just did not permit it. The soldiers and constabulary were easily recognized by their uniforms, and those not in uniform still maintained that military bearing recognizable from miles away. Peasants and farmers were the most poorly dressed and often did not have any footwear. If they did, it was so shoddy that they would have been better off without.

As Daniel became part of the mob, he kept a wary eye on those nondescript citizens. They were dangerous. The nondescripts most often were the thieves and pickpockets who made a living off of crowds. As dangerous as the thieves and pickpockets were, Daniel was not as concerned about them as he was about the spies and assassins who lurked about in the shadows or disguised themselves as peasants, noblemen, or merchants.

Eventually, he made his way through the gates. The heat and stench of the big city smacked him in the face like a wet rag. Galway reeked, but this was unbearable. Galway's stench dissipated quickly due to its openness, but Dublin was surrounded by high walls and opened only to the docks at the far side of the city. The heat and stench of thousands of people lingered in the air for a long time. It settled and seethed into the dirt below and mixed with older stenches from years past, only to be stirred up by the thousands of pairs of feet that trudged through the city streets each day. This reason alone explained why Dubliners and visitors preferred a windy, rainy day.

He recovered and pressed on toward the marketplace,

where numerous merchants attempted to sell their wares and goods. However, this was not the marketplace Daniel sought. There was a more sinister marketplace within these walls that very few knew about. Those who did know were not the type to trust. An illegal slave trade of children and women within the very heart of Dublin existed. As much as Daniel did not wish to admit it, he knew Cassandra must have passed through Dublin and may be waiting to be bought on the slave market.

A peasant woman bumped into him. "Excuse me sir."

Daniel rubbed his left hand where he felt a slight burning sensation. He staggered slightly. He lost his focus. He felt nauseated and became dizzy and disoriented, and then he vomited. He had been poisoned. Daniel stumbled into an alley and held himself up by his right hand as he vomited violently. He was incapacitated and vulnerable. He reached for the opal around his neck. Passersby ignored him, as they only saw another drunk who could not hold his ale.

Daniel turned the opal over in his hand. Between expulsions, he licked the back of the opal. After his fifth lick, he regained his poise. As he did, a greasy burlap bag was pulled down over his head. He was seized by both arms and dragged down the alley. Daniel thought, *It must have been the woman. I have been so preoccupied with looking for men that I forgot that women also have been employed as assassins, but not by any factions in the West. They have only been utilized by sultanates of the Ottoman Empire. Why would Eastern sultanates have an interest in me? I must not let my captors know I took an antidote.* Daniel resisted ever slightly while giving the guise of faint resistance and allowed himself to be dragged away. He collapsed every thirty feet or so to maintain the ruse.

"Athair, the knight has been gone a long time—several hours," Brian said, pacing back and forth.

"I know. Precisely three hours and twenty four minutes."

"What? How do you do that? Never mind. It's a long time. He should have returned by now."

Athair nodded and stood up from his meditating position. He looked at Brian but then turned toward Balor and Macha. Both acted nervous. Balor marked his territory more than usual, and Athair heard low whimpers as the mastiff made his rounds. Macha stopped grazing and scraped the ground with her front hooves.

"Yes, Brian, perhaps you are right. Balor and Macha are nervous also. Something is wrong. Animals sense things differently than we do, especially Balor and Macha. They are so attuned to their master that they feel when something is not right."

"Okay, then let's get down there and see what's going on."

"Not yet. There is much to consider."

"Come on. He could be dead or captured by now. What's to consider?"

"My young friend, you have not learned anything in the time you have spent with the Opal Knight. Several concerns must be considered. First, we don't know he is in the city even though that is the last place we saw him when he entered the gates. He could have easily been smuggled out among any of the merchant carts leaving the city. Second, we do not know the force we are up against. It could be a few to a hundred. Third, and most importantly, when we find him, how do we free him? He will certainly be under guard. Do you have the answers to any of those concerns I addressed?" Athair asked, knowing the answer.

Brian stopped pacing to look at Athair, shook his head, and then faced the city. He took a deep breath and sighed to himself, feeling helpless. Athair walked over next to him, with Balor and Macha flanking the two. Athair placed a hand on Brian's shoulder.

"You act tough, but you do care about him, don't you?"

Brian just looked down into Athair's eyes and answered without opening his mouth. He owed the knight more than Athair knew, even more than Daniel knew.

"We will get him back," Athair continued. "We shall wait until dusk, just before the gates are locked for the night."

Daniel continued to allow himself to be dragged through the streets. Even though the cover over his head was burlap, Daniel was still able to see shapes and light. He knew the sun would descend soon. He felt anxious about the darkness, but if he was not left alone, he might be able to get through the night without a huge fire. There was always ambient light available in large cities such as this, but would it be enough?

Michael and John discussed what they knew had to be true. They acquired two horses bred for speed and took off at a ferocious pace toward Dublin. It would be just before morning before they arrived to warn Daniel that he was headed into a trap.

As dusk neared, Athair and Brian headed toward the

city gates. They hid all of the armor and most of the heavy weapons. Brian tore his clothes and rolled around in the dirt, grass, and even some dung. Athair did not change his appearance. They did not want to appear to be a threat. They were just a monk riding a horse with his pupil alongside. The pupil led the horse, with his master atop and their faithful dog alongside. They appeared destitute and would escape any scrutiny because of the common knowledge that all monks loved animals. That's why the dog and horse appeared in better condition than the men. They neared the gates and entered with just a passing glance by the guards. The changing of the guard was about to occur, and the outgoing guards did not want to waste time on two filthy peasants. Athair and Brian continued to walk toward the center of the city.

"Well, we are in. What's next?" Brian whispered, looking up toward Athair.

"I am not as adept at tactics as the Opal Knight is. However, I have been alongside him in several of his campaigns and have picked up some techniques. One, we will use shortly."

Michael and John pushed their horses hard for several hours. They were more than halfway to their destination when the lead horse carrying John slowed. He realized that he had pushed his mount toward its death and reined him in. Michael pulled up alongside, and they both dismounted. They needed new horses quickly. At the rate they had pushed the horses and the urgency of their mission, these horses would not last another hour without their hearts exploding within their chests. Villages dotted the highway every five to ten miles, but they could not just barge into a stable and take horses. Stealing was not an option, regardless of the magnitude of the situation.

Daniel's captors dragged Daniel down some broken stone steps. He counted twenty in all, not including the two landings. Wherever they were going, it was not good. The smell of human waste and rotting food hung in the air. The clanging of weapons, probably short swords, and the clinging of keys certainly indicated that they were in a dungeon or prison, but he was unaware of any such prison located underground in Dublin. He had heard that Dublin was built upon ancient burial sites. *Is it possible that these tombs were converted into jail cells?* Daniel felt the rhythm of his heartbeat increase as his anxiety grew. He tried to remain calm. The burlap bag was removed from his head as his captors shoved him into a cell. Traditional prison cells were barred on two or three sides, with the fourth section and ceiling of the cell made of stone. Oddly, this cell was centered in a small room. It was barred on all four sides and the top. The only stone section of the cell was the floor.

A lone figure stepped from the shadows. Daniel's mouth widened in shock.

The End

ABOUT THE AUTHOR

My entire life, I have been fascinated by history. When I discovered my great-grandfather's memoirs dating back to before the Irish Potato Famine, I began to have daydreams about what it was like living in Ireland during those times.

I was born and raised in the Bronx, New York. I attended a Catholic grammar school for eight years, a Catholic high school for four years, and Fordham University for two years. Fordham University is a Jesuit school. It is quite obvious that my formative years were heavily influenced by the Catholic Church. I ran cross country and track all four years in high school and one season at Fordham.

At the age of nineteen, I enlisted in the US Army as an artilleryman in 1983. My first duty assignment was in the Federal Republic of Germany (West Germany). I spent seven years in West Germany and witnessed the collapse of the Berlin Wall along with communist influence in Europe. I was selected to be a recruiter and then assigned to Fort Drum, New York. Five years at Fort Bragg, North Carolina, soon followed, with my final assignment being teaching leadership for three years at the University of Idaho Army ROTC. I retired as a first sergeant. I am currently an instructor for leadership for a major transportation company. Married with two children, I have coached Little League baseball and soccer and have also been involved in Scouts. I am a past master for my lodge of Free and Accepted Masons.

The Irish have always been considered great storytellers, and I have used that influence to teach. This story has been running over and over in my mind for many years.